ASTROTURF

ASTROTURF

Matthew Sperling

riverrun

First published in Great Britain in 2018 by

riverrun

An imprint of

Quercus Editions Limited
Carmelite House
50 Victoria Embankment
London EC4Y 0DZ

An Hachette UK company

A CIP catalogue record for this book is available from the British Library

Hardback ISBN 978 1 78747 115 3

10 9 8 7 6 5 4 3 2 1

Typeset by Jouve (UK), Milton Keynes

Printed and bound in Great Britain by Clays Ltd, Elcograf S.p.A.

for K.A.

I

NED LEARNED HOW TO do intramuscular injections from YouTube. The most helpful video, made by a Californian anti-ageing clinic, began with a doctor in a white lab coat making a speech to camera about the beneficial effects of testosterone, and solemnly saying that these drugs should never be used unsupervised, without a doctor's prescription or for recreational purposes. He brought on an assistant, a young man in underpants and a vest. The young man's head was cropped out of the shot as he stood next to the sitting doctor. The doctor said that he was going to demonstrate the technique with a sterile saline solution. He held up a syringe containing an inch of orange liquid. To inject into the quadriceps muscle, he said, you divide the front of the thigh into four quadrants by drawing lines up and across the middle of the leg, then inject into the muscle at its thickest point in the quadrant closest to the hip. He took a felt tip pen from the pocket of his lab coat, drew the lines on the man's leg, picked up the syringe again, uncapped the needle, took the barrel between his thumb and first finger like a dart, pushed it into the man's thigh with a swift action, plunged down with his thumb so that the orange liquid disappeared in a second, and pulled the syringe out. It looked simple.

Ned had watched this video five or six times. Before he found it, he had watched several series of webcam diaries documenting the hormone therapy of people transitioning from female to male, and as he worked his way through the videos over a few hours, he watched them becoming androgenised week by week, injection by injection, developing beards and muscles and Adam's apples. The videos moved him, and he was moved too by the community of supporters who offered their encouragement, shared their own experience of transition, and gave praise and feedback in the comment section below each video.

Now he had everything in place, laid out on the desk next to his laptop: the needles and syringes in their paper and plastic sleeves, the vials of yellow liquid, the box of anti-bacterial wipes. He clicked on 'Play again' and tried to breathe deeply in through his nose while he watched the demonstration video once more; by the time the video finished, he felt calm and slightly light-headed. He went to the sink in the corner of his bedsit, washed his hands, looked at himself in the mirror, and sat down again. One millilitre of oil, containing 250 milligrams of Testosterone Enanthate: it didn't look like much, when Ned had drawn it up into the syringe using a thick, nineteen-gauge needle. He twisted that needle off and replaced it with a fresh, twenty-five-gauge needle – the thicker needle to draw the oil with, the thinner needle to inject with – before warming up the oil in the barrel by wafting a lighter under it for a few seconds, and tapping out the air bubbles.

He had decided to pin his right quadriceps. With his jeans around his ankles, he tore open a wipe and swabbed the injection site; the smell of alcohol rose from the wipe while the hair on his thigh became slicked down in swirling patterns. He picked up the syringe, uncapped the needle, and for the next five minutes held it against the skin on his thigh, afraid to push through. Sweat gathered on his temples. He needed to think of it in more practical terms, he told himself; remember how the doctor had just darted it in, with no more difficulty than if he were pushing a cocktail stick into a cherry tomato. That was the state of mind Ned needed to be in: as if he were carrying out a simple mechanical operation, using materials whose properties and behaviour were known and predictable. Never mind that one of the materials was part of his body. He had read a dozen times on the forums that there were no nerve endings inside muscle tissue. He should barely feel anything.

Ned took a deep breath down into his belly and out through his mouth, pinched an inch of skin and fat between thumb and finger with his left hand, and with his right hand pushed the needle in. There was a sharp sting as it broke the surface of the skin, then nothing. The needle sank into the muscle smoothly and Ned continued pushing until it was entirely sunk into his thigh, an inch and a half deep. He let go of the syringe so that it hung out of him and stood up independently. It looked like he had a strange new appendage, a lever or prong, added to his body.

He had read about the importance of aspirating the injection, to check you hadn't hit a blood vessel. The thought of a plume of blood bursting into the barrel made his heart pound, but when he pulled back the plunger only a clear bubble of air appeared. With his thumb he started to work the plunger down. It surprised him how hard he had to push. The thick oil passed through the thin needle slowly, and by the time the barrel was empty he had been pushing down for what felt like a whole minute. His hands were shaking, causing him to stir the needle in the muscle. Finally the black plug of the plunger met the bottom of the syringe, with all the golden oil gone. Ned whipped the pin out fast and felt his thigh ache. He imagined he could feel the oil within the muscle, a little pocket of liquid nestled an inch and a half inside of him. A bleb of crimson had come up at the injection site. Ned wiped it off; the alcohol in the swab stung.

TWO WEEKS EARLIER, IN mid-January, he had been walking past the dry cleaner on the high street on a Saturday morning, looking at the people queuing up outside the fancy new coffee shop he hadn't visited yet, when he was arrested by a familiar voice. '*Yo, Ned!*'

Ned turned to see Darus removing and coiling up his earphones while holding the phone they were plugged into and an empty smoothie cup in one hand and three shopping bags in the other. Darus was smiling, but the sight of him gave Ned the guilty feeling that this was somebody he had let down, who was disappointed in him, and whose text messages he hadn't replied to. It was the first time they had seen each other in more than a year.

They went into the coffee shop. When they had ordered and sat down, Darus said, 'So what happened? With your training, I mean? It seemed like you were enjoying the gym so much at the beginning.'

'Well, you know, I suppose I lost a bit of motivation. I mean, I enjoyed it, but it's just . . . when I saw myself in the mirror after six months of pretty regular training and there was nothing – I was still so skinny – I felt like my body just didn't want to do it.' Darus looked like he was waiting for more, and Ned added, 'The money got to be a bit much, as well. Thirty-five pounds a week is not nothing.'

Ned could feel Darus's scepticism. He was anticipating a reply along the lines of 'And how much do you spend every week buying sandwiches from the coffee shop, instead of making your own?', but instead Darus said, 'We could've worked something out with the money. I'm just sorry to hear that you lost your motivation, because that's my job as a trainer, to keep that up. I used to see you sometimes when I was training other people and I could tell that you weren't completing your routines. Sitting there between sets staring off into space. So I feel bad now that I didn't do enough to keep you on track.'

'Oh, it wasn't your fault,' Ned said. 'I'm always starting new things and then letting them slide. It's just the way I am, I can't keep up with anything that feels, you know . . . regimented.'

Darus's nostrils flared a little in response, and Ned felt himself cringe. The first time they met, Darus had told him how much he hated it when people said they couldn't stick to an exercise programme because they weren't 'that sort of person'. It meant they had given up on themselves. Ned had the sense this was a speech Darus had given many times.

'No, I'm a great believer in people's capacity for change,' he said, his eyes shining with defiance – as if Ned had accused him of not believing in that. They had only been talking for five minutes. Darus had fallen into conversation with Ned as he stood by the filing cabinet where the work-out programme cards were stored, and at first Ned had thought that the heavily muscled guy covered in tattoos with the intense manner was simply being friendly. Even when Darus suggested that they could train together and he could show Ned how to improve his work-out routines, it took Ned a minute or two to realise he was proposing that he pay him for it.

Ned had been briefly energised by Darus, by his conviction that everyone had the capacity to decide how he or she wanted to behave. He had stuck to the work-out programme Darus gave him for a few months, and had lost the excess body fat that he put on in his late twenties, the years of sitting at a computer all day with his shoulders slumped forward, eating scotch eggs. But when he missed a few sessions, it felt like all the advances he had made would slip away almost instantly. Inexorably, listlessly, he had dropped off from his routines, and within a few more weeks had stopped training altogether, and started ignoring the messages Darus sent over the next few months. Soon he had let his gym membership lapse altogether.

Sitting here in the coffee shop a year later, Darus didn't seem to bear a grudge. He sipped his flat white and said, 'It's probably true you don't have the genetics for getting big. You're always going to be a hard gainer. But that doesn't mean you should give up on training altogether. Were you putting creatine in your protein shakes?'

'Yeah, right from the beginning, but I didn't really feel any difference.'

'Hmmm. Well, I hope you decide to come back to it one day, and I'd love to train you again if you do.'

'Cheers, man. I'll think about it.'

A pause. Darus had twisted the sugar sachet into a ribbon between his fingers. He looked up and met Ned's eye. 'You know, there is another option for low-T guys like you.'

'What's low-T?'

'Testosterone. That's why you don't have any muscle mass.'

Ned bristled slightly at the suggestion. 'How do you mean?'

'If you have more of it, your muscles can absorb more protein. That's why guys have naturally different body types, it's how much testosterone your body produced when you were growing up. If I met your dad and your brothers, I bet they'd have the same build as you, right? Skinny arms, tall and thin, narrow shoulders?'

'I don't have any brothers,' Ned said.

'But your dad is like that, right? So that's just your genetics. That's what you're working with. And even if you trained like a beast six days a week and ate all the protein in the world, you still wouldn't get big. You can make some gains, but there's only so much.'

'Right. It's depressing, isn't it?' Ned said.

'But what I'm saying is, there is another option. You can give your genetics a boost.'

'Like what?'

Darus leaned in across the table, checking with his eyes that they weren't being overheard. 'You remember Charlie from the gym, right? The trainer with those veins that bulged out of his arms? How do you think he got like that?'

'I'm not sure.'

'Well, what do you think about the guys you pass in the street who make you shrink back when they walk past, and you just know your girl is looking at them? Basically the guys like me, I mean.'

'I'm not sure –' Ned said.

'Okay, let's say this is the jungle. You'd be a beta male, right? No offence, but that's just scientific fact. Right now I mean the guys who'd be the alpha males in the pack.'

'Yeah?'

'Let me tell you, it might be natural for a few of them, but the other seventy-five, maybe eighty per cent of those guys are on steroids. When you turn on the Premiership and they take their shirts off and they're completely ripped, not a shred of fat on them, sixty per cent of those guys have been on steroids in the off-season as well. When you see pretty-boy actors with those big fucking arms swelling out of their t-shirts, and when you see squaddies hauling their big backpacks on the train, 100 per cent of those guys are on steroids. Everyone in the film industry knows it, everyone in the military knows it. But no-one admits it.'

'So what are you saying?'

'I'm not suggesting anything. I'm just saying, if you wanted to know how to give your training a boost, I could tell you how to run a cycle where after ten days you'd just feel, like, *Grrrrrrrr!*' (Here Darus sat back, brought his clenched fists together in front of his body, tensed his chest and biceps and set his face in a snarl, showing his teeth.) 'You'd feel like a fucking grizzly bear ready to rip somebody's head off with your bare hands. And you'd be smashing those pull-ups and chin-ups, then be ready to do another set with twenty kilograms strapped around your waist. It can't work miracles, but after sixteen weeks, if you're training and eating right, you could look like . . . well, like someone who's still tall and lean but is on the way to getting seriously ripped as well. Someone with some power in their arms. And you'd feel different.'

'Isn't it illegal?' Ned said.

'Nah, hardly: over here, it's like class-C drugs or some shit. The same as prescription medicines. So no-one gives a shit unless you're literally dealing it to schoolkids in huge quantities.'

'But isn't it dangerous?'

'Look, I'm not going to push it on you or anything. You've got it use it right, but if you do, it's amazing stuff, and honestly I recommend it just as a health product for almost anybody. Here . . .'

Darus reached into the pocket of his tracksuit bottoms for his phone, tapped at its screen with his thumb, and said, 'Go here and read the threads that are pinned up at the top of the forums. They're called, like, "Information for newbies" or "Introduction" or something like that.'

Five seconds later, Ned felt his own phone twitch in his pocket.

THE TEXT MESSAGE THAT Darus had sent Ned in the coffee shop said 'Roidsweb.com.' That evening, Ned clicked on the link and found himself looking at a forum that must have been set up ten or more years ago; its grid of boxes reminded Ned of the football fan forums on which he used to read transfer gossip when he was at university. He left the window open, clicked back to his home screen and immediately forgot about it.

Six days later in the pub after work, when the rest of the Chevron Web Solutions team had gone home and only the two of them were left, Piotr asked Ned why he had broken up with Grace a few months previously. Piotr had liked Grace, he said, although as far as Ned could recall they had only met twice. Ned was taken aback by the directness of the question. None of his English friends, and none of his other colleagues, would have asked him that, Ned felt; it was another sign of what an interesting person Piotr was.

'She broke up with me, to be honest,' Ned said.

'I'm sorry to hear that. It had been a couple of years, right?'

'Oh, it's okay. I mean, I don't think she was the love of

my life or anything. But I thought things were going okay between us.'

'So did she say why she was breaking up with you?'

'Yeah, but it didn't really make that much sense. I think she thought we're not well matched enough in terms of our characters. Like, I'm too negative and pessimistic, and she wants to be with someone more optimistic. I think she might have met someone else, to be honest; it sounded like she was just casting around to come up with some reason.'

Piotr left a pause. 'Did *you* think you were well matched?'

'Not exactly. But when she says I'm pessimistic, what it really means is that I'm *realistic* but I haven't grown up in this world where absolutely everything is entitled to me on a plate.'

As he heard himself say this, Ned became aware that he was feeling a little drunk.

'So you were divided by the famous English class system,' Piotr said. 'And she doesn't think you're confident enough? You're too much thinking the worst is going to happen, so you don't try things?'

'That's part of it, I suppose.'

Piotr shrugged. 'It sounds like maybe you were not well matched. But it may be you could learn something from her attitude. The people who are totally unafraid of failing because they always expect success, you know, they're the people who get things done. If I had thought "There's no point trying for my computer science degree at the same time as while I'm working full-time, it'll be too much hard work, blah blah blah", I would never have tried and I wouldn't be here now.'

'It's not like I'm constantly going around the place thinking, "I'm going to fail".'

'No, not constantly. But I think you are a little bit lacking confidence, as Grace says.'

Ned thought about this while he stood at the bar waiting to buy another round of drinks. From anyone else, he might have found it insulting, but Piotr had a knack for saying things in an even-handed, forthright way, so that they seemed disinterested and constructive. These qualities made Piotr a good manager, Ned thought. They also must have served him well in his online life; he had recently told Ned about his activities under the handle XTRMNTR on Reddit, Twitter and 4chan, where he was an authoritative commentator on cultural myths. Ned looked it up as soon as Piotr told him, and found himself compulsively reading everything XTRMNTR had published. He found some of the opinions about men's rights and so on rather hard to take, but in others he could see the sense, such as when Piotr argued that the so-called 'feminist' arguments against pornography actually restricted women's sexual expression.

Piotr hadn't told anybody else in the office except Ned about XTRMNTR – neither the owners of Chevron nor the other people Piotr managed – and Ned felt privileged to be let into this aspect of his life. XTRMNTR had almost 20,000 Twitter followers, and seemed to deal with a constant stream of interactions from them. Ned was surprised that Piotr could manage to do all this while still getting his work done; creating XTRMNTR's online content seemed like a full-time job in itself, as far as he could see. Maybe Piotr was just more energetic than he was.

It took Ned a long time to get served. Piotr was right, he thought: it was confidence that held him back. Maybe Piotr was right about him and Grace. When Ned thought about it, it was painful to remember what his feelings had really been during his relationship with Grace. He had gone from finding her only moderately attractive when they first met, to acting like he was slavishly grateful for the fact that she had become his girlfriend, even when it turned out that she was never very nice to him. She was always finding faults in his manner of dress, his taste in food and movies, or the things he would say when they were talking to other people, especially her friends. It made him self-conscious, but if he ever tried to defend himself, or mention something in Grace's behaviour that he didn't like, she would become crazily indignant and say he was attacking her. From a few months into their relationship, Ned had an ever-running internal monologue of resentment and sarcasm going in his head when he spent time with Grace. And yet he was unable to break up with her. It fell to her to do it, and when she did, he felt terribly rejected. He even asked her to take him back: the thought of it drew a wince from him now. Just at that moment the barmaid met his eye. 'I'm doing my best here,' she said, and Ned said, 'Oh no, sorry, I wasn't making that face about you.' At least he would get some drinks.

Two pints further into the evening, Ned and Piotr got to talking about sex, and Ned said, 'That was another thing with Grace – the sex was a bit crap, to be honest.'

'Ah!' Piotr said. 'Now we get on to the real reasons for why you broke up.'

Ned laughed. 'No, not really, but it was just . . .' He looked around to check there was no-one within earshot, and leaned in closer to Piotr. 'I always found her attractive, and she has this amazing figure, but it's like there was something a bit prissy about her attitude to sex. Like she finds it all a bit icky, but goes through with it out of goodwill.'

'Prissy and icky, you're testing my vocabulary here but none of that sounds very good.'

To Ned, it felt illicit and liberating to tell these things to somebody else; he had rarely spoken like this about his own life to anyone before. He leaned in closer and was almost whispering. 'The thing was, she never let me do anal with her. I wanted to, but she would just say, in this sort of babyish voice, "That's where poo comes out of". But then one day she told me that she used to do it quite often with her ex. And that just drove me crazy. I couldn't get it out of my head, this thought of what he had been allowed but I wasn't.'

Piotr put one of his large hands firmly on Ned's shoulder. 'It sounds like you should've been the one breaking up with her. If she wouldn't give you her arse but she did it for someone else, it just means she didn't respect you. She didn't think you're a man.'

'Hmmm. I don't know about that,' Ned said.

ON THE BUS HOME from the pub, Ned thought back to the conversation three months earlier during which Grace had broken up with him. It was last October. They had met at a coffee shop near Grace's flat – an odd choice for a meeting-place, he thought, since they had never been there together before. When he entered, he saw her across the room with her head bent over a book.

'Whatcha reading?' he asked.

Grace looked up from what turned out, on closer inspection, to be a notebook. 'Hello. You're late. I was just doing my accounts actually. I'm totally broke.'

Ned draped his jacket over the back of the chair and held back from saying, *Yeah, broke apart from the flat in Brixton that your parents bought for you* . . . Grace didn't have a job, except for the few days a month of volunteer work she did at a charity supporting the rights of Palestinians. Her main thing was her art, but Ned couldn't recall her selling any of her pieces in the time they'd been together. In truth, Ned could make almost nothing of the monochrome abstract paintings that Grace was now creating. When they first got together, he found some pleasure in talking to her about her work, and was proud to have a girlfriend who was an aspiring artist. It made him feel that he was back in touch with his younger self, the person he had been when he did his degree, read classic novels and occasionally went to exhibitions. But somewhere along the way, his ability to be interested in her work had run out. Now he looked at Grace's paintings and had nothing to say, paralysed by his anxious feeling that either he wasn't clever enough to get it, or Grace was having him on. Surely all she had done was cover the canvas entirely, if unevenly, with a single colour . . . but then how did that justify her habit of giving the paintings titles from works of political theory ('The Working-Day', 'Dialectic of Enlightenment')? Ned went through phases of finding it amusing, baffling and irritating – but was mostly in a phase of irritation these days.

'There could be worse situations, you know,' he said, 'than getting to spend your days making art and listening to Radio Four. Some of us have to go out to an office all day. And pay rent.'

Grace looked at him as if she were talking to a child. 'I have to pay a shitload of fees to the property company, you know. And the leasehold will need renewing in a few years. It's not exactly a goldmine.'

'Well, sure, but—'

'Will you just fuck off with this stuff for today, Ned?'

Ned spread his hands to say *Fine*. It was not the first time they'd had this conversation. Since he learned, early on in their relationship, that Grace owned her flat outright, he often found the fact coming to his mind. A few weeks earlier than that, one of the Chevron co-owners had told him he'd bought a three-bedroom house in Southwark ('Where did you get the money for that?' Ned had asked, and Alex said with a wink, 'Not through the sweat of my brow, old boy'), and in the same month, two of Ned's friends from university days, Eric and Katy, had bought a terrace house in Bow with the help of a huge deposit from their parents. To Ned, it felt like the world was shifting: one moment he thought the people in his circle were all modestly getting by, and the next it turned out that many of them had been rich all along. He had the feeling of being left behind. He was still living at the limit of his overdraft at the end of every month, as he had been since he was eighteen. He had only started earning enough to be paying back his student loan four years ago, and the bedsit that he rented for slightly more than half his net income verged on being squalid. In a large house already divided into five flats, the landlord had turned the basement utility rooms into bedsits with a shared kitchen and bathroom. The water pipes for the whole building ran through Ned's room; whenever anyone showered, flushed the toilet or ran the tap, the sound of their waste water coursed through the pipes three feet from where he lay his head at night. The shared kitchen and bathroom had no natural light, and the bedsit only had a single square window that looked out onto a brick dug-out below street level.

'I wanted to . . . There's something . . . Ned, are you even listening?'

Ned looked up from the menu.

'I wanted you to meet me here instead of coming round or going to the pub,' Grace carried on, 'because I thought we should do this soberly. I've been thinking about it a lot, and actually I think we should stop seeing each other. We can still see each other as friends, if you'd like, but that's all.'

It took Ned a few seconds to process the fact that he was being dumped. He scrambled to adjust. He told Grace that it was fine, they could just be friends, and heard his voice come out flat and toneless.

'Do you even want to know why I think we're not good for each other?'

'Okay. Tell me.'

'It's like, one thing is your attitude. How you're always being so snarky and resentful. Even now, when you brought up my flat, I could hear the jealousy in your voice. And fine, my parents are rich, I'm not going to apologise for that. Some people have been more fortunate than you. But it's like you use it as an excuse to not even try doing anything for yourself. You'd rather sit there and snark at other people. You don't help yourself, and because you're so caught up in negativity, you give it off as a vibe and it puts people off you.'

Ned pondered this for a few seconds, and asked, 'Who does it put off?'

'Well, like . . . my friends, for instance. I don't know if you've noticed that we haven't been hanging out with my friends together as a couple recently, but it's because I know that if we do, you're always going to start on about how stupid someone is. And usually it will be someone who's really good friends with one of the people you're talking to. Meanwhile you just sit there like you're Mr Superior and you're so clever . . .' The tears that Grace had been holding back broke out. 'I said I wouldn't cry, but it just upsets me, it upsets me to see you like this. I want you to be a happier person, I want you to be better, but I feel like I don't know how to help you.'

She was crying copiously now.

'Are you even going to say anything, Ned?'

Ned was suddenly hungry: he ordered eggs royale and a glass of homemade lemonade, and when it arrived he set to eating wolfishly.

WHEN NED GOT BACK to the bedsit after his evening with Piotr in the pub, he flicked indifferently through various websites before going back to Roidsweb and looking again at the introductory threads on the Steroids Q & A forum in the Community section of the site. It held his attention; as he read, he felt himself sobering up. His reading confirmed what Darus had told him: testosterone was at the heart of the matter. Higher testosterone levels promoted increases in lean body mass by allowing more effective protein synthesis within muscle tissue, and it was protein synthesis that allowed broken-down fibres to repair themselves and thus to grow bigger. At the gym, people tried to cause small tears in their muscle fibres so that the muscles would increase in size when they repaired themselves.

The more notes Ned took, the more sense it made. What if the thing that had always been holding him back was not, as he had thought, his shyness or his tendency to sabotage himself, but rather the lack of vigour, the diminished assertiveness, the tendency to fatigue, that were associated with low testosterone? Admittedly, he had never suffered erectile dysfunction except when very drunk, and his beard grew fairly thickly. But who was to say what range of testosterone levels was normal and what was deficient? The way people on the forum talked about the transformations they could make in their physiques, the elation and euphoria they felt when they were on cycle, and their increased assertiveness and drive . . . – why should Ned go on passively accepting the limits of his body?

Before Darus had made his suggestion, Ned was perhaps already susceptible to the idea of using drugs to change your capacities. When he first drank alcohol as a teenager, the effect was magical and immediate: after two tins of lager, he felt like a different person, and the world seemed rich and thrilling, as if time had started moving twice as quickly. Talking to people was easy; he was funny, relaxed and charming. That night stayed with him as a luminous memory, but it became harder to recapture as he started drinking more in his late teens. Then in his mid-twenties when he had first started as a web developer, he had briefly used Modafinil, a wakefulness agent that heightened his powers of concentration and his mental stamina. Suddenly Ned could wake at six in the morning, go jogging before breakfast, and concentrate unbrokenly at work, going straight through until evening. His code became a bit cleaner; he could answer more emails per day, as if his concentration had narrowed to a tightly focussed beam of light. But after three or four weeks, the effect seemed to wear off: he had to increase the dose, and this made him grind his teeth and feel withdrawn and robotic when he spoke to people. Even when he was on the drug, the old problems returned: the sense of indecisiveness, inability, low spirits. The spell was broken.

It seemed like steroids were different though. They could have long-lasting effects. It was clear that brain activity had a major effect on hormone production: testosterone levels raised in response to moods, thoughts and other external stimuli; they raised when you had sex or when you thought about it; they raised when you felt aggressive or were put in a situation of confrontation. And so it was also clear to Ned that certain experiences of his teenage years had not just resulted from, but contributed to, his relatively low levels of testosterone. It was obvious, if you thought about it. Why were the bullied kids, the geeks and nerds, inevitably physically weedy, or prone to retaining body fat like a woman? It wasn't just because they were picked on for their already-existing weediness or fatness, but because being bullied had a symbiotic relationship to their weediness. It made them weedier by inhibiting the working of their brain, their pituitary gland and their hormone system. Ned remembered the morning in his fourteenth year when, late for class, he had hurried across the carpark to where the rest of his year were filing into the assembly hall, and Nathan Garner shouted *You're walking like a bender!*, so that fifty pairs of eyes turned to look at him and that word – *bender, bender* – clung to him for the next six months . . . He was right back in the moment: the feeling of the mind shutting down, his ability to think being inhibited by self-consciousness and fear. Of course it was the cause of a physical shrinking-away too. It all made sense. But it could be reversed.

The most helpful thread Ned found on Roidsweb was entitled 'NEWBIE MUST READ: Beginners first cycle protocol'. The initial post had been rated more highly than any other on the forum. The thread continued for seventeen pages, most of which were taken up with comments praising the wisdom of this first post, and it had been pinned to the top of the forum. It explained in great detail how to run your first steroid cycle over a period of twelve weeks, followed by three weeks of post-cycle therapy. By the time Ned had finished reading, he realised with surprise that it was four o'clock in the morning. He logged into his email, deleted some junk messages, and composed a new message to Darus. The message included the link to the beginners' cycle thread, and said that Ned was thinking of following its instructions. He got up, cricked his neck, went for a piss and crashed into bed.

When Ned's alarm woke him at 7:30, he felt groggy and dehydrated. Taking up his phone, he found an email reply from Darus:

> Sounds fucken awesome bro. I'm just jealous I can't go back in time and have my first cycle over again. Hit it hard bro. Darus.

Ned made himself a strong coffee and went back to the laptop. The ordering instructions were a little complicated, but within a few minutes he had ordered two vials of Testosterone Enanthate and a bottle of Nolvadex from one of the most highly rated suppliers on Roidsweb and a quantity of syringes and needles from another website. After that he went back to bed. It was Saturday morning.

THE DAYS OF WAITING for his gear to arrive had been agonising. Ned could hardly concentrate on his work for wondering whether his package would arrive, the police would knock on his door, he would get a seizure notice saying his package had been confiscated at the post office, or there would be nothing at all, just silence. Perhaps what he had done was crazy. He had made an illegal order of controlled pharmaceuticals, probably manufactured in an unlicensed underground lab, from an anonymous middleman. He had wired off £130 in cash to someone who, for all he knew, might not even exist. He was completely at their mercy if they wanted to send him nothing, ignore his emails of protest, blackmail him . . . – his mind worked eagerly with disastrous scenarios.

Yet when Ned considered the matter calmly, the nature of the Roidsweb community gave him confidence. He spent more time on the site in the days following his order, digesting a large amount of information and becoming familiar with all the major personalities on the forums. There seemed to be hundreds or even thousands of people who had taken the same risks as him and had nothing go wrong. The supplier he had ordered from was well trusted; the customer service experience had been exactly as the forums said: prompt, courteous and – except for having to pay by cash transfer rather than through a bank – completely professional.

On the fifth day after he had placed his order, a small brown jiffy bag plopped through his letterbox onto the mat, with no return address. It looked totally innocuous.

NED FELT NO DIFFERENT after pinning for the first time. His thigh ached dully, even after he took a warm shower and massaged the muscle in slow circles. After two days, three days, it still felt like nothing was happening. He almost lost patience and injected for a second time, thinking that he hadn't used enough, or that his gear was under-dosed, but his better judgment told him to remember what the forums said: it would take a week and a half for the body's hormone levels to rise in response to the new chemicals in his system. He simply had to wait it out, to eat healthily, and drink plenty of water.

On the fourth day, he realised that his mood had changed. When his alarm went off in the morning he felt alert and clear-headed, and didn't press snooze even once. His cock was very hard, despite the fact he had masturbated twice the previous evening. He got straight out of bed and was breakfasted, showered and dressed within fifteen minutes of waking. As he walked to work, his mind felt lucid and free of anxiety. He wanted to see people, to experience the city, and he felt in harmony with its rhythms. His steps felt light, his feet springing up from the pavement. He couldn't say what was different, except that he felt present in his body in a way he hadn't before.

In the office he was on top of his game. He dealt with a string of client queries decisively and courteously; he solved a refactoring problem that had been festering for almost a fortnight, coming up with an elegant solution that cut through a tangle of code; and at lunchtime he came out on top in an argument with his colleagues about which of the *Godfather* films was the best. In the afternoon, when Piotr turned to their colleague Robin, nodded in the direction of Ned's fluorescent green polo shirt and loudly speculated that Ned had come to work dressed as a tennis ball, and Robin asked Ned if any dogs had chased him on the way to the office, Ned shot back with, 'I think that says more about you, Piotr; you've got balls on the brain, you're seeing them everywhere you look.' Robin shouted 'Wahey!' and Piotr grudgingly rose to move the banter trophy from his own desk over to Ned's, where it remained for the rest of the day.

That evening, Ned had a training session with Darus. It was a legs and shoulders day, the days that Ned had previously disliked, but once he had warmed up on the rowing machine he felt focussed and strong. While Darus prepared a barbell in the squat rack, hoisting up the twenty-kilogram plates and loading them on, Ned shook his legs to loosen the muscles.

'I've put eighty K on there,' Darus said. 'See how you go with that. First superset is squat, shoulder press, jump squat, lateral raise. Three sets of ten reps each, and concentrate on your form. The important thing on the squats is to go deep, get your butt level with your knees before you start back up.'

Ned's previous maximum squat for three sets was sixty-five kilograms, and at that weight he would feel his knees and ankles wobbling on the last reps as if he might topple over. He walked under the bar, positioned his shoulders in the middle so that he could feel the cold metal against the base of his neck, lined up his hands on the bar at shoulder width, gripped hard, squeezed his core muscles, braced against the bar and pressed upwards, trying to stand up straight. It was easy – barely more difficult than standing up with a rucksack on his back. He stood in front of the mirror with his back straight and his shoulder blades pinned together and took a deep breath, filling his lungs as much as he could and enjoying how the bar gently rose and sank down.

'Now let's blast out ten reps. Come on, Ned!'

Watching himself in the mirror, and keeping the bar steady, Ned started to bend his knees. He couldn't believe how firmly in control of the weight he felt. He got cleanly all the way down, so that his thighs were parallel to the floor, held the weight there for a second, felt the pressure building in his thighs, then pushed up through his heels, feet, legs, glutes and core until he was standing up straight again.

'Yeah, you're a machine!' Darus said.

The next nine reps were almost as easy. By the tenth, Ned could feel the burn in his thighs and hamstrings enough to know that three sets would exhaust the muscles nicely. After forty-five seconds' rest, he did ten seated shoulder presses with a fifteen-kilogram dumbbell in each hand, ten jump squats, where he stood on a mat and jumped upright as explosively as he could from a deep squatting position, and ten lateral shoulder raises with the ten-kilogram dumbbells – all of them weights heavier than he'd used before, and yet weights that he could now manage comfortably. On the second and third supersets, he circuited back round through these four exercises, feeling his muscles burn satisfyingly, needing a few swigs of water and a few pauses for recovery, but still feeling a conviction that amazed him. Darus spotted for him on the heavy reps, keeping him from flagging and getting up in his face like a drill-sergeant – 'Come on, bud, squeeze out two more now, drive, drive' – so that Ned could smell the dinner on his breath.

Ned's second superset consisted of leg presses, barbell shrugs, calf raises and reverse flyes; his third consisted of leg curls, front shoulder raises, hamstring curls and rotator cuff pull-downs. By the end of the last rep on the final set he could barely stand. His heart was thumping, his head was light, his quadriceps and hamstring muscles had melted, and his hands hurt so much he couldn't get his training gloves off without Darus's help. His grip was cramping up. His vest was soaked in sweat down the middle of his chest and back, but he didn't mind. For the first time, it felt like he could do it; he could be one of the men at the gym whose lifts earned the respect of the lifters he respected.

'You did good today,' Darus said at the end of the session. 'Took quite a beating, huh? You were hitting it hard, but you need to be doing that every time if you're gonna make the most of this. It's time to step up to the plate, because now's your chance to be in the big league, bro. Where we play with live rounds.'

WHILE NED WAS ON cycle, lifting felt euphoric. He was able to push himself as hard when he went to the gym on his own as he did when Darus trained him. He was going to the gym four times a week: he would see Darus for a chest-and-back day, then come in on his own for legs-and-shoulders, then arms, then another chest-and-back day, before seeing Darus again for a leg-and-shoulders day, and so on. Each time he increased the weights he was lifting and each time he found he could master the new weight, keep good form and hit his muscles hard. When he did a chest-and-back work-out and was on his last set of incline chest flyes, lying on his back on the sloping bench with twenty-four-kilogram dumbbells in each hand, he would take the weight down low, so that his arms were fully spread and his elbows were lower than his chest, and would squeeze, bringing it back past the point where it felt like his pectorals were about to shear off from his sternum and his arms were going to rip from his shoulders, then would push through the burn and finish the set before collapsing, totally spent.

He felt like his arms, chest and back were somebody else's. When he bench-pressed, he felt like there was an invisible pair of hands supporting his elbows and pushing them up. Weights on which he would previously have wobbled and halted mid-lift were weights he could now smash through to the top of the rep, then lower down with strong control to full extension and smash upwards again. He started moaning and grunting as he lifted. Within a month he could do twenty wide-grip pull-ups without a pause.

Darus sent Ned a YouTube clip that showed Arnold Schwarzenegger in *Pumping Iron* talking about the feeling of a 'pump': when he had just finished an exercise and massive levels of blood were rushing into his swollen muscles, so it felt like his skin was going to explode. 'It's as satisfying to me as coming is, you know, as having sex with a woman and coming,' he said, in his thick Austrian accent. 'So can you believe how much I am in heaven? I am getting the feeling of coming in the gym; I am getting the feeling of coming at home; I am getting the feeling of coming backstage when I pump up; when I pose out in front of five thousand people, I get the same feeling. So I am coming day and night. I mean, it's terrific, right?' Ned was starting to understand what Schwarzenegger meant. After a work-out, Ned would crawl to the locker room and collapse on the bench, feeling loopy, light-headed and barely able to move.

And his body was changing. Within a fortnight, his abdominals were visible, the skin was tight across them and the ridges of muscle cast shadows across his body in the dim lighting of the basement changing room. His shoulders were getting broader; his lats were thickening; his pectoral muscles were becoming thick and shapely, and now almost disguised the slight depression in the middle of his chest by pulling his rib-cage into position. The veins in his forearms looked swollen and vaguely obscene. When he bent his arm, his biceps tensed to a hard, round peak, the skin tight across the muscle; when his arm hung loose at his side, it felt strong and substantial. His body was becoming substantial. He was becoming solid.

ONE LUNCHTIME, NED LEFT work to go to Ryman's. The tatty cardboard box he had been sent by the needle exchange didn't seem good enough anymore. In its place, he chose a shining red metal moneybox with a lock. It looked like a toy sports car. He took it home that evening, packed his vials, needles, syringes and swabs into it, locked it up and put it under his bed. An hour later he found himself getting it out, unlocking it and looking at all the things again. The vials seemed to be enchanted objects; he held them up to the lamp so the bubbles and thicknesses in the oil were delicately suspended in golden light, felt how the glass became warm in his hands, and placed them against his lips.

Ned didn't talk to anyone except Darus about his gear at first. He only used it when he was alone in his bedsit with the curtains closed and his phone on silent. He enjoyed the secrecy. He had split his dose into two injections, to keep his levels stable, so he pinned half on Wednesday and half on Saturday. After a few weeks, the moment when he had to break the skin with the needle was no longer difficult.

On Roidsweb, Ned progressed from lurking to making contributions of his own. He started a thread entitled 'First Cycle', where he gave a brief introduction to his training history, described his plan and narrated his training sessions and injections. The other forum members were supportive. *DWhite* wrote: 'Awww boy, nothing like a first cycle! First cycle and first time getting your dick sucked, the two best moments in a man's life. Good luck with it, chief.' *Carsten* wrote: 'Sounds like a well-researched plan – great to see a new member who's prepared to do some learning before they begin.' And *Rooneyboy* wrote: 'Great results already, you're clearly very responsive to gear. Don't be afraid to push your lifts even harder. Go hard or go home, is my motto.' Ned found himself obsessively refreshing his browser window, until he had to ration it: he told himself he would only check for new messages after every ten queries he answered at work. The messages kept coming.

The warmth of the forum members settled Ned's doubts about what he was doing. The more he learned about steroids, the more he understood how wrong their reputation in the wider world was. Why shouldn't somebody use a synthesised version of a chemical that was already present in their body? Why shouldn't somebody seek to optimise the way their body worked?

So far Ned had only run through these arguments in his

head, arguing his case in front of an imaginary audience. But in the third week of his cycle, when Ned took off his sweatshirt while he was standing in the work kitchen after lunch waiting for water in the coffee machine to heat up, Piotr looked approvingly at his arms and said, 'You've stepped up your training routine?'

'Yeah,' Ned said, 'I've been putting more effort in. It dropped off last year but I've got back on it in the last couple of months.'

'It looks like it's really paying off.'

'Thanks, man.'

'How are your routines different? Are you doing more compound exercises like I was telling you?'

'Yeah, I'm doing plenty of that, and building it into supersets so that I'm basically doing interval training at the same time as lifting. You know, no rest between sets.'

'Aha,' said Piotr knowingly. 'And are you taking any supplements?'

Ned looked at him. He knew that Piotr had a fair bit of gym experience, and he knew from his XTRMNTR posts how open-minded he was; in some of them, he had argued for the complete legalisation of drugs. He was a rational sceptic, averse to received opinions – that was his whole thing. So surely it would be okay to let him in on it. Ned felt it rise in him as a physical urge, almost irresistibly, to share the secret with somebody else. A couple of seconds had passed.

'At the moment I'm on creatine, whey protein and a little bit of test,' Ned said, as casually as he could.

'Oh, like a test booster, you mean?'

'Yeah, sure, just a little bit of testosterone to optimise recovery and muscle growth.'

Piotr had been reaching into the fridge, sorting through the expired plastic bottles of milk, his back to Ned, but now he turned round. 'You mean you're taking hormone supplements?'

'Well, yeah, I suppose.'

'Don't you think that's a little bit unnatural?'

'Not really, no – testosterone is naturally present in the body, so all you're doing is optimising the amount of it that's available for muscle recovery.'

'But it's cheating, Ned. Surely that's obvious.'

'Why? I mean, if I was a professional athlete, sure, it would be against regulations. But everyone knows they're totally arbitrary.'

'It's interfering with your natural level of ability. That's why it's immoral.'

Ned sighed. He had read these arguments so many times, and they were so wrong-headed, that he had his rebuttal rehearsed already.

'If anything it's the opposite, Piotr – it makes sporting competition fairer if performance enhancers are allowed, because—'

'Oh, come on, Ned!'

'No, hear me out, it makes it fairer because it creates a level playing field between people who happen to be born with exceptional genetic gifts and people who don't. It equalises that difference. So now someone who's naturally quite slender can start on a more level footing with someone who's naturally muscular, and it just comes down to how hard they train and how smart and disciplined they are.'

Piotr was thinking. 'You have this all worked out, huh?'

'Well, I've thought about it a lot. In fact, I don't even like to talk about it as equalising people's natural capabilities, because when you look into it they're not really natural at all – they're totally shaped by upbringing and environment and diet and all that stuff.'

Piotr put the steam nozzle into his jug of milk and caused it to emit a loud rush of noise. When he turned around again he raised his eyebrows, said, 'It all sounds very postmodern, but I think I am not persuaded,' and walked out of the kitchen. Ned was disappointed that the argument had ended so quickly, but knew that he had won.

As his cycle progressed, Ned felt the benefits of his increasing strength flowing into the rest of his life. As long as he was hitting it hard in the gym, none of the things that had previously made him unhappy mattered. In fact, they didn't even seem to be the case anymore: he now regarded his colleagues and clients with an amused, level, fond, sympathetic gaze. His new discipline and well-being meant he was drinking very little and cooking for himself more often, and therefore spending less money on food and drink and finding that he did, in fact, have enough money to live on. And he seemed to have a different effect on people. People who had known him for a long time gave him quizzical looks, surprised by his new energy and optimism. His pub-going friends made sarcastic remarks about how he wasn't so much fun anymore since he didn't want to get drunk with them in the middle of the week, but Ned could tell that really they were envious. They felt bad because they no longer had him as an alibi for their own depression and self-pity. People who had seemed to disapprove of him, especially women, now looked at Ned as if they had noticed something new. He would see it happening: a flicker of confusion and a half-smile would play across their faces, followed by a warm, attentive gaze.

One evening in late February, the fifth week of his cycle, Ned was walking home from the gym when he heard a woman's voice say his name. He peered through the gloom at a couple stalled on the central reservation, fifteen feet away. As they walked towards him, the man doggedly kept his arm around the woman while she turned and said something quietly to him. They got closer and their faces grew distinct. Grace!

'Hello,' Ned said, and leaned in to kiss her on both cheeks.

'You're out late,' said Grace. She nodded towards the huge gym bag slung over his shoulder. 'You look like a burglar.'

Ned laughed. 'Casing a few joints. Have you been out?'

'Just to Short Stack for a drink. Umm, Ned, this is Federico. Sorry, I should have introduced you. Actually, you might have met before.'

Ned shook the man's hand, gripping firmly. He looked like one of Grace's graduate student friends, with a ratty ponytail and a receding hairline, and Ned sensed him shrink back when Ned said, with an enthusiasm that must have struck him as slightly deranged, 'How are *you*, Federico?'

'I am well,' Federico said, with what Ned took to be the studied awkward dignity of a man meeting someone who has fucked his girlfriend more times than he has.

'What do you do?'

'I'm working on neoliberalism and its effect on societal bonds, writing about my own country, Chile—'

'Right, yes,' Ned said. Now he remembered having met Federico: it was at the birthday party of another of Grace's graduate friends, where Ned had got very drunk and ended up stuck in a corner with this bore who gave him a ten-minute lecture about his thesis topic. And Grace was dating him – the thought of it was hilarious.

Ned looked at Grace. She looked rather tired, bundled into a shapeless black duffel coat that flattened her breasts into a single bulge and made her look short and blockish. 'We should catch up one day,' she said. 'You're looking very well. Have you become some sort of fitness freak?' She made a mime of squaring up her shoulders and puffing out her chest like a robin.

'I've been back in the gym. *Mens sana* and all that. Yeah, we should catch up – why don't you give me a text when you're in the neighbourhood next time and we can go for coffee? I'm still on the same phone number.'

'Okay, that would be great,' she said. 'And it's really good to see you looking so, umm, fashionable.'

Ned laughed; he was wearing a plain, maroon t-shirt and a grey hoodie that had both come from Primark, with some old jeans and trainers. *Fashionable*: he took it to be Grace's confused way of saying she found him attractive in a way that she didn't quite understand. Her gaze lingered, smiling, on his face for a second too long, and Federico looked annoyed. Ned put him out of his misery by telling them that he ought to get to bed.

When Ned got home, he flicked through nude photos of Grace on his phone while idly stroking his cock until he fell asleep.

THE IRONY OF NED'S raising his testosterone levels was that it temporarily caused his testicles to shrink. The exogenous testosterone he put into his body made his hormone system detect that no more was needed, and his endogenous testosterone production paused. Ned was prepared for this; he had read enough about 'shutdown' to know that his balls would return to normal at the end of his cycle, as long as he got his Post-Cycle Therapy programme right. But it was disconcerting. Ned had been checking in the shower each day, and although there was no single moment at which he could mark shutdown as having occurred, by the fourth week his balls definitely seemed less plump and firm. It was mainly noticeable when he was cold, or when he was very turned on: his scrotum seemed to gather into his body more tightly than normal, with the skin hard and intricately wrinkled like a walnut shell. The first time he masturbated after shutdown, he wondered whether his load would be smaller – he had read people on the forums saying that it might be – but he didn't find this to be the case.

The weirdness of testicular shutdown was counteracted

by the huge swelling of desire that he felt while on cycle. It seemed to spread out from the seat of his body, from his prostate up through his spine and belly and out to his fingertips, toes and the top of his head. He felt like his cock was constantly hard, or like his whole body had an erection; like the unspoken presence of sex was an electric charge in the atmosphere, so that other people could pick it up off him. In this state he liked to stroke his cock but stop just shy of coming, repeatedly getting near to orgasm, his brain blazing and moronic with sex, then stay there, slowly letting the climax recede until it came back stronger an hour later. It felt like a source of strength. Ned remembered reading somewhere that before a fight boxers would abstain from orgasm for six weeks. He had found it outlandish: the longest he had gone since he was thirteen years old without wanking or having sex was probably no more than two or three days. But now Ned felt like he understood it. It made him more focussed, to retain rather than disperse his powers. Pretty soon he hadn't come in almost two weeks.

EARLY IN THE EIGHTH week of his cycle, Ned had reached the end of a chest-and-back training session during which he had bench-pressed over 100 kilograms for the first time ever, and was sitting with Darus by the gym's reception area, drinking his protein shake and feeling pumped and light-headed from the work-out.

'You're looking pretty fucking cut these days, you know,' Darus said. 'I wouldn't be surprised if the guys upstairs asked you to be in one of their campaigns soon.'

'What campaigns?'

'You know those films they have playing on the TV loop in there? It comes on about 9 a.m. and 4 p.m. each day, where they have the SunFit Success Stories. They show some skinny dude or some fat whale of a girl for the "before" shot, and it's horribly lit with the room all messy, like a terrible amateur photo. Then they show a professional photo for the "after" shot, where they're flashing their abs and they're suddenly suntanned and dressed much sexier. And they interview the people about their transformation.'

'I dunno, man. I mean, I'm flattered and everything.'

'Well, I'm not saying they would ask you yet. You've got a long way to go. But it's something to aim for. I was thinking how cool it would be to have it written at the bottom of the screen, like "Ned, 30, computer programmer, trained by Darus Gaynesford's Super Beast Training, TM".'

Ned laughed. He still found it hard to tell when Darus was joking and when he was in earnest. 'I'm a web developer more than a programmer really,' he said. 'But I'll keep it in mind as a goal.'

Darus lowered his voice. 'How long you got left on cycle?'

'Four weeks.'

'And you've got your PCT meds all lined up, ready to go?'

'Oh yeah, I ordered those at the beginning.'

'Awesome. Sides under control? No hair loss or, like, trouble peeing? No gyno?'

'Nothing.'

'It feels fucking awesome, right?' Darus said. 'I'm planning another cycle for the early summer and I'm already feeling like my mouth is watering for it, like I'm just gimme gimme gimme.'

They sat in silence for a few seconds, watching two hard-bodied girls filing past in high-tech fabrics and fiddling with their phones. When the girls were out of earshot, Ned said, 'Have you got your gear for the summer cycle lined up already?'

'Some of it, but not all,' Darus said. 'I'm going to be stacking a few different compounds, with some orals as well, so it's a bit more complicated. I've got the orals but I'm looking for a better source for injectables. My last source sent me stuff that turned out to be bunk.'

'How did you know? Did you test it?'

'You just have to inject that shit and see what the effect is. There's always a window when you're not sure if the gear's bunk, because your hormone levels might not adjust for like two weeks, and if you're stacking more than one, you can't know which of them is having the effect.'

'Right, I see.'

'If any dealer wants to scam people, they can just put cooking oil in some vials and sell that shit as the finest Trenbolone, and by the time people realise it's bunk, they'll be long gone. And I really can't afford to be wasting any money right now. Which reminds me, you haven't paid me for this month's sessions yet.'

'Oh, shit. Sorry about that.'

'No biggie. It's just that I'm pretty fucking squeezed at the moment. Did you know that the club has raised its fee for trainers from 500 to 750 pounds? It's fucking outrageous.'

'What sort of fee?'

'The trainers are self-employed. We pay SunFit 750 a month just for the right to train people in their club. It fucking sucks. It means I don't get national insurance. If I get sick, I don't get anything.'

'Shit, man. That's awful. I didn't realise.'

'Well, don't worry about it.'

NED WAS GOING TO the gym five days a week now, only taking Wednesdays and Saturdays off. He was still relatively slender among the gym members who used the free-weights area, but now his frame was intricately sheathed in lean muscle. His shoulders were a few inches broader, his chest and back were thicker and his torso widened into a V-shape from a narrow waist, with every part of his body distinct and cabled. He could load up three times his body weight on the leg press and shift it like it was nothing; he was benching one and a half times his body weight.

He felt like he was learning about his own capacities. He knew now that there were stages of muscle pain through which one had to pass. When he was doing preacher curls, with enough plates loaded onto the EZ-bar that it was as heavy as he could lift while keeping good form, he would encounter the first stage after seven or eight reps. It came as the beginning of a burning sensation in the thickest part of the biceps, and brought an awareness that he would be more comfortable if he stopped. When he resisted this impulse, he pushed on towards the second stage, which came towards the end of the second set. The pain changed to a flickering sensation, as if flames were licking at the fibres in his biceps, coming and going in intensity. The desire to stop the exercise had to be strongly counteracted at this stage. Ned found it best not to distract himself but rather to try to inhabit the pain, to observe it with curiosity and to accept it. When he pushed on, if he had judged the weight correctly, he met the third stage as he approached the final reps in his third set. By now the burn was constant and was spreading to other muscles; the pressure in his abdominals, forearms and shoulders, which were supporting the lift, was growing intense. The burning in his biceps became the focus of his being, with his whole consciousness narrowed down to those two small groups of muscles. They felt so tight and hotly engorged that they might burst open as he counted out the final reps and reached failure, with the EZ-bar wobbling in mid-lift, before he somehow found energy he didn't think he had, smashed his hands back towards his shoulders so the bar swung to the top of its arc, and the set was finished. At which point he racked the bar and flopped across the bench, unable to move for several seconds.

Ned realised that the point wasn't the lifts themselves; the point was to create an occasion for an encounter with his own limitations. Success was achieved by pushing his muscles to the point of failure; coming up against his limits was the way to push his limits further in the next session. He trained with a steady faith that what seemed like an unliftable weight today would be looked back on fondly in the weeks to come, when he had surpassed it.

On a Wednesday afternoon in the ninth week of his cycle in late March, he was sitting in the office, sipping water and working his way steadily through a backlog of emails, when he found himself with no unread messages for the first time in ages, looked at his watch and realised it was an hour later than he thought. He had worked his way through all the emails in an unbroken burst of absorption, his mind clear and responsive. Now he had paused, he could feel the pleasant tiredness in his muscles and the blood softly pulsing inside his ear. An immense calm came over him. His body felt lit up and free of cares. He concentrated on his breathing, to try to draw the moment out, went into a sort of meditative state, and realised that he felt unreservedly happy.

2

THERE WERE TWO WAYS to gain kudos on Roidsweb. The first was to show yourself to be expert in the Community section: to make authoritative contributions to technical discussions and help other forum members with their cycles and training programmes. The second was to make notable contributions to the Off Topic board, where members talked about sex and relationships, politics and the financial crisis, music and films and TV. They shared jokes and funny videos; they asked for advice and sought sponsorship for half-marathons. Off Topic was the busiest part of the website.

Ned was doing his best at appearing expert. He was a fast learner, but some forum members had been involved with bodybuilding for twenty years. He decided to dedicate half his time to the Off Topic board and half to the other boards, trying to make several comments, from as many of his accounts as he could, on each discussion that was underway. At any time he would have as many as twenty separate incognito browser windows open on his laptop, each one logged in to a different account.

When he felt confident enough, Ned began starting new discussion threads of his own. Writing as *Big Squid* from Miami, he entered the title 'When you're called out for being a juicer at your mom's dinner table', and wrote:

> Hey bros. So I went to my mom's place for easter (not a christian, we just like to get the family together), and everybody ate and got pretty drunk. Things took a weird turn when my cousins start making funny remarks about how I didn't look "natural" like I was going to explode. Normally I take this as a compliment, it means my training is working and I look like the baddest mofo I can be, but I mean when my cousins and my brothers are saying it and my mom's right there looking worried? I just sat and took it and got hella drunk to numb it out, but I was wondering if anybody else experience the same things at parties with people who don't know what it's all about. Advise on how to respond would be appreciated. Okay rant over.

He waited a minute, changed to the window where he had *Mr Reptilian* logged in, and wrote this reply:

> feel 4 u guy. i decided last year to be full on honest and explain how I feel steroids are a great choice with many benefits for anti-ageing and health if used responsibly.

> some people still look at you like you're a junkie but that's they're ignorance and deep down they're prolly jealous of your physique and the hard work and self discipline it shows. so that's why they try to flip the script on you but fuck that shit, stay strong bro!

By the time Ned had finished writing this comment, *Big Squid*'s original post had received five up-votes, and had been replied to by two other posters with messages of support. He logged in as *FilaXL* and quickly wrote 'mad props to reptilian speaking some proper wisdom there'. As more real posters came to comment on the thread, he kept the conversation lively by chiming in from different accounts, adding more stories of what it's like to interact with people when you're a juicer: how you deal with it towards your family, whether you tell your girlfriends or hide it from them, and so on. He used his sockpuppets to up-rate each other's posts too, so the kudos was constantly building for all of them. The highest-rated post came from *Castle Greyskull*:

> The way I see it is, a juicer has to mann up and be open with there family otherwise there living a lie. If your girl can't except your choices you make as an adult then she shouldn't be in your life. More difficult with the Mums but I maintain that you can't live your life wanting everyone to

approve of everything you do. Tell her the truth, explain how you know what your doing and let her handle it or not.

That seemed to settle the matter, and the thread was dying out, with replies slowing to a trickle. Ned went back to the window where he was logged in as *Big Squid* and replied to *Castle Greyskull*, 'sure thing bro but I'm pretty sure my mom's way of handling it would be to shop me to LE', then he went back to the window where he was logged in as *Castle Greyskull* and replied, 'i'm guessing law enforcement don't care about chasing a juicer just cos some old girl says her sons got big guns'. Back once again to *Big Squid*: 'lol you're prolly rite bro'.

Ned gave himself a short break after that.

ALONG WITH THE COMMUNITY section, the other half of Roidsweb was the Source Reviews section. The front page of Source Reviews presented a huge table with the names of different steroid suppliers down the left-hand column and, next to them, ratings out of 100 for Service, Delivery, Pricing, Quality and Overall. Clicking on a supplier name led to an individual supplier page with a link to their website and a review thread where members would give ratings and comments on the transaction. Other forum members, including the supplier themselves, could reply to that review, and also rate it.

Roidsweb sold nothing; it was a platform that allowed suppliers to connect to consumers. It didn't take a commission on sales. Supplier membership and user membership were free, and the only way the site made money was by running adverts at the edge of the screen and in between forum posts. Ned was delighted by the purity of the idea behind the website. It was a self-organised community of risk and trust. A supplier's success was based on their history of completing orders professionally and in good faith, and the status of the members was determined by the ratings of their fellow members.

If Ned's plan was going to work, he needed something to sell. Steroids for injection came with the chemical dissolved in oil, and the most common carrier oils were normal domestic ones; from the Health and Personal Care department on Amazon, Ned bought grapeseed oil in two five-litre bottles for £17 each with free delivery. That would fill 1000 vials with 10 ml each, he reckoned. He went to an online medical supplies store and ordered 1000 glass vials with butyl rubber stoppers and metal vial tops, along with two pairs of vial crimpers and 500 amber pill bottles with child-resistant caps. Then he did a run around all the chemists and pharmacies in town, buying as much generic aspirin as he was allowed from each. He could fill each bottle with fifty unmarked tablets, which cost less than half a penny per tablet, and sell them, marked up as Nolvadex and Clomid, for £50 a bottle.

Ned knew that packaging was crucial, and approached the design task with great care. The brief was to create labelling for vials, cardboard boxes and pill bottles which would be consistent with the website design and compliment slips, with a clean-edged, sterile, professional look. After several drafts, he settled on a sky-blue and white theme with diagonal lines cutting across the horizontal axis on which the text was set. It looked beautiful, and worked nicely across the whole range of labels, boxes and letter-heads. He uploaded the design to Vistaprint and found, after a little poking around, that he could also buy silver hologram stickers to make the vials and bottles look extra-authentic.

When it arrived, he put everything out on the kitchen table and got a one-man assembly line going: he suckered up 10 ml of oil with a syringe, squirted it into each bottle, popped in the rubber stoppers, crimped the metal vial tops, stuck on the labels – being sure to line them up straight and press them onto the bottles with no wrinkles – constructed the cardboard boxes from the flat nets, stuck a sticker and a hologram on each box, boxed up the bottles and lined them up in a tray. When he had filled, stoppered, crimped, labelled and boxed two hundred bottles, he paused to admire his handiwork. It had taken an hour. The boxes looked terrific, lined up like toy soldiers. The silver holograms were an excellent touch.

The final thing Ned needed was an identity card to collect the payments with. After one of his sessions with Darus, he asked him whether he knew the best way to obtain a convincing fake ID. Darus smiled widely at him. 'What are you up to?'

'Oh, you know, I just thought it would be useful to have

one,' Ned said. Darus made a face, and Ned said, 'Okay, the real reason is that it would make me feel safer ordering gear if it didn't come in my own name. If I'm not at home to collect the parcel, which I'm usually not, I have to go and pick it up from the post office and I'd rather not be doing that under my real name.'

'I think you're probably worrying about nothing,' Darus said. 'But if it really matters to you, I could probably help. Do you use Bitcoin?'

'I haven't, but I know about it.'

'That's the way to get one that looks real, to get it from Silk Road on Tor. But if you've never done it before, you could give me the cash and I could sort it out for you.'

'No, I could manage that. Do you know how much it would be?'

'I dunno, I'm guessing maybe fifty quid.'

Within two days, the fake ID had been ordered. Ned had everything he needed to run a one-stop steroid shop that could fill several thousand orders, and his overheads barely amounted to £400.

NED HAD REACHED THE end of his first cycle three weeks before he set his scheme in motion. Twenty-four times in the twelve weeks previous to that, he had pinned his left or right thigh or gluteal muscle with Testosterone Enanthate; for the next week he had injected a small amount of Human chorionic gonadotrophin subcutaneously every day, using an insulin pin which he slid into the fat beneath the skin next to his belly button; and for the next two weeks, he had taken Nolvadex to complete his Post-Cycle Therapy. He felt fine. He hadn't experienced the slump that people on the forums warned about when they stopped pinning; his energy levels, strength and mood felt consistent as the gear left his body. He pictured a star system overlaid on his frame, its points of light fading out one by one as the half-lives of the steroid molecules ended.

The experience had changed his relation to the whole world of objects and forces. He inhabited his body more fully, with a heightened awareness of its muscles and joints and their interactions, and he had a finer sense of the points at which its edges met the world. Taking a walk or sitting still in a chair, he truly felt how matter pressed in on him. His touch met objects with a new grace and recognition, as if he knew their heft and purchase, their biting points and centres of gravity, for the first time.

Since finishing his cycle, Ned had gone easier on his training. He still made it to the gym at least twice a week, and did chin-ups, press-ups, planks, and crunches at home on the other days, but he reduced his sessions with Darus to once a fortnight. Darus still emailed links about fitness, motivation and diet. His new obsession was with the myth that high cholesterol was bad for you; Ned received a lot of information about that. But Ned ignored Darus's calls to get in the gym and hit it harder. His aim had never been serious bodybuilding; he just wanted to feel stronger and better. He did. He was in the best shape he'd ever been, and he found that he could maintain it with three trips to the gym a week.

His PCT period coincided with the coming of a warm late spring, and he loved the feeling of his arms and shoulder swelling out the sleeves of a t-shirt. Ned felt like his first cycle had had a permanent effect, not just on his physique but on his state of mind. He had retained the mental gains – he might even say 'spiritual' gains – that it had given him. None of the depression, self-thwarting or lack of vigour that he had experienced in the first thirty years of his life returned; when he looked back, they seemed like the experiences of a different person. He left his window and curtains open at night so that when he awoke, the light and the fresh, ozony smell of the air were pouring into the room already. He tried to take a walk in the park each day while the sun was out. The grass was absurdly bright green; the girls came out in bikini tops and denim shorts. Life was good.

As Ned sat on the sofa in his bedsit one Saturday morning, eating his bowl of raw porridge oats, protein powder and a sliced banana with milk, the feeling of the sun streaming through the window across his face was strangely sensuous and he became aware that he had an erection, pushing uncomfortably against his tracksuit bottoms. He found himself vividly taken up by a memory: Grace was underneath him with her knees pulled up and resting against his chest, and he was fucking her slowly, watching his cock moving in and out of her shiny cunt, and she was saying, 'Here, let me', taking his cock out and stroking him decisively with her hand while looking up with amused eyes and saying, 'Are you going to come?', until he shot his load across her belly, and she looked down, grinned and said in a small voice, 'Gosh, it's a lot . . . '

Ned heard himself give out a groan. It was the first time in ages he had thought about Grace. When was the last time he had even touched, been touched by another person? It was only Darus in the gym, supporting his elbows if they were giving out during dumbbell chest presses. Or it was Ned accidentally brushing his fingers against the palm of the girl in the newsagent as he handed her coins. He was briefly tempted to have a wank there and then, just for the release, but he thought it would put him in the wrong mood for the gym, too passive and slack.

A FEW DAYS LATER, NED was leaving the gym when the hot girl who spent all her time on the cross-trainers – now wearing a slouchy get-up of jogging bottoms and pink t-shirt, her hair still wet from the shower – smiled at him in the reception area. He smiled back and was surprised when she said, 'Is it Ned?'

'Yeah. Hello.'

'It's Alice? I'm a friend of Grace's?'

At once, Ned remembered: he had been to Alice's birthday party two years ago; she was a friend of Grace's from their undergraduate days. In the run-up to the party, Ned had been rather dreading it, since Grace's account of Alice gave such a negative impression that he didn't understand why they were going to the party at all. As far as Ned could tell, Grace's relationship with Alice was comprised of her rolling her eyes at anything Alice posted on Facebook, sarcastically parroting it to Ned in a whiny drawl as he sat at the other end of the sofa. And yet when they arrived at the party, Grace made a beeline for Alice and hugged her closely for two or three seconds. Ned had been primed to meet somebody self-absorbed and unreflectingly, brashly posh, but instead he found Alice graceful, funny, modest and interested in other people. They had a five-minute conversation during which she seemed genuinely fascinated by Ned's work, and afterwards Ned felt truly seen and acknowledged. She was lovely. In addition to which, she really was exceptionally hot, in the peculiar way that only posh English girls could be. It wasn't hard to see why other women might have complicated feelings about her. She had been the theatrical star of Grace's undergraduate year-group, and was working as an actress and model when Ned had gone to her birthday party – a failed actress, Grace would always say, living off her parents' money. When Ned mentioned on the way home from the party how much he had liked meeting her, Grace said that of course, Alice was fabulous, she had always said so. And here she was now, standing in front of Ned at the gym, where he must have seen her frequently in the period since her birthday party without recognising her.

'Alice, of course. How are you? It's been such a long time.'

'I'm good, how are you and Grace?'

'I'm great, and I think Grace is well too, but we split up a while ago.'

'Oh, no, I didn't know that,' she said, and touched Ned's arm with her hand. 'How are you feeling about that?'

'Oh, fine.'

'Good. I'm glad to hear it. You look like you're in great shape.'

Her hand was still resting on Ned's bicep; he leaned into it slightly as he shifted towards her.

'Thank you. You too. Well, you always have.'

Alice looked herself over and shrugged. 'Are you still working in web development?'

'Yep,' Ned said. 'Let me know if you ever need a website doing.'

'I'll bear it in mind. It must be very interesting, understanding all the nuts and bolts of the internet.'

'It's not without interest.'

'Ha!' She laughed as keenly as if he had actually made a joke, then took half a step closer to him. With her hand still on his arm, she met Ned's eye with her face tilted downwards, her gaze cast up and a slight smile playing across her lips. 'You mustn't tell anybody this,' she said, 'but my membership's actually expired. I don't know why my card still works in the turnstyle thingy. I'm getting a freebie at the moment.'

Ned mimed zipping his lips shut.

'Look, I've got to go and meet somebody,' Alice said. She opened her handbag, pulled out a huge stack of flyers and worked the top one free from the rubber band. 'But I'm in a play this weekend, if you'd like to come.'

It was for a production of *Doctor Faustus*, and it showed a tall, slender woman with brown hair, her face turned away from the camera and her body thinly covered by a gauzy dress. Ned could make out her breasts and a shadow of pubic hair.

'Who do you play?'

'Helen of Troy. A non-speaking role. I'm just doing it to help out a friend really,' she said. 'I'd love to see you there. Now I need to go and dispose of the rest of these.'

She looked down at the stack of perhaps 1,000 flyers in her hand with puzzlement – whether at the oddness of carrying around 1,000 near-naked pictures and handing them out to strangers, or in amusement at a person such as herself being asked to perform the menial work of distributing flyers, Ned wasn't sure.

WHEN NED AND PIOTR entered the room above the pub where the play was taking place, they were each handed a programme printed on a sheet of folded A4 paper. The back page had the opening speech of the play on it. After looking at it for thirty seconds, Piotr turned to Ned.

'*Shortly he was graced with doctor's name*, it says. So I'm spending my Friday night, when I should be in the pub, watching a play about a doctor?'

'He's a scholar studying magic,' said Ned, who had looked at Wikipedia that afternoon. 'Just wait for it to start.'

Piotr looked pained. 'I know I'm not going to understand this. One, I'm a computer scientist, not a literary person. Two, it's written in some kind of nineteenth-century English. What the fuck?'

'Sixteenth-century, actually.'

'Jesus!'

'Look, if it's awful you can just leave. It won't be long anyway. I think they're going to run through to the end with no interval.'

But when the play began, Ned too found it baffling, almost incomprehensible. As a student he had surely read lots of books with language as archaic as this, but a decade on, he was totally lost; just when he thought he had the gist of what one character had said to another, the way the other character acted in response seemed to totally contradict his idea, and he was back to square one. The main character, Faustus, spent half his time seated at a school desk piled with dog-eared science textbooks, pretending to read. He was dressed as a modern-day student, in Converse trainers, a black hoodie and low-slung jeans with his wallet on a chain hanging from his belt loop. Every now and then a man holding a video camera backed onto the stage, followed by a heavily made-up blonde girl in a trouser-suit who held a microphone to her mouth and ploddingly gave a sort of commentary on the action, then shifted from her stilted poetry voice into a slick presenter's voice to say, 'This is Laura Jones reporting for Al-Jazeera from Wittenberg, Germany'.

The highlight came when Alice walked out from the wings across the stage like a catwalk model, in a white dress and high heels, with her head held imperiously high; at the edge of stage left she turned, pausing to face the audience for a moment, then walked back the way she had come. A few minutes later she came out again; the guy playing

Dr Faustus kissed her and fell to his knees in front of her, and they left together hand in hand. He looked out of his depth. In heels, she was taller than he was.

Before the play was over, Piotr rose from his seat and whispered to Ned that he would be downstairs in the pub, and the moment the applause started, Ned joined him. As they stood there drinking pints of watery lager, the cast and crew came in. It was odd to see them back in civilian life, no longer spot-lit on stage but about to fade into the crowd. Members of the audience came up to offer them congratulations and drinks. Ned couldn't see Alice yet.

'So how far have you got with her?' Piotr asked.

'Oh, nowhere yet – we just bumped into each other at the gym, and we slightly knew each other already, and she asked if I wanted to come along to this.'

'Right. But you made a move on her, yeah?'

'I said I'd come along to her play.'

'Okay. That's not the ideal move but it's a start.'

'Piotr, I'm not going to start using your rules-of-the-game bollocks when I talk to people.'

'You wouldn't say it was bollocks if you'd seen how much pussy it could get you.'

'I'm doing alright for myself as it is, thanks.'

'I say nothing. Just promise me you're going to fuck her, okay.'

'I would certainly like that to happen.'

'I think you would be making the trade of the century, to get dumped by Grace and start fucking Alice.'

'It's not a fantasy league team, Piotr.'

'It would be like trading an out-of-form Rooney for a fit Messi.'

'Well, I wouldn't want to fuck either of them.'

Piotr laughed, clinked glasses with Ned and said he would get the next round in. While he was at the bar, Alice caught Ned's eye, waved theatrically ('Coo-ey!') and walked over.

'Congratulations,' Ned said. 'I thought you were excellent. Everyone was.'

'Thank you. I certainly managed not to fall over. Or to laugh while they all debated how hot I am.'

Ned laughed. 'It's nice that you filled the room.'

'God knows what they came for. I suppose the design was nice. Obviously they put my tits on the flyer for artistic reasons.'

Alice laughed smokily at her own joke and Ned raised his eyebrows at her, fixing his gaze on her face. Piotr came back from the bar and handed Ned his pint. With nowhere to rest it, Ned stood holding pint glasses in both hands, and he knew exactly what Piotr was about to say, his pub catchphrase for whenever anyone had two drinks on the go, which

Piotr duly said: 'Double fisting, eh?' It made Ned wish that he could talk to Alice alone, but to his surprise, she sniggered, looked at Ned and said, 'With *your* reputation?' They all laughed.

'He is a very dark horse, this one,' Piotr said. Ned gave him a shut-the-fuck-up look, and Piotr grinned. They talked about the production, and Ned was relieved when Alice admitted that she too found some of the language in the play difficult to follow. Piotr jumped in with, 'Personally I have no fucking idea what was going on up there,' but Alice looked disappointed at his going this far.

'It's powerful though, isn't it?' Ned offered – 'all that poetry, even if you don't know what it means.'

'Exactly,' Alice said. 'That's just how I feel. Even if you don't understand the literal sense of a speech, you *understand* it on a different level because the poetry just sort of conveys it in images.'

This perhaps wasn't quite what Ned had meant, but Alice's intent gaze, as she elaborated on his suggestion, seemed to be retrospectively transforming his experience of the play. He preferred this new account of what he had been going through in the room upstairs, built up in collaboration with Alice, to the impatient boredom he had actually been experiencing thirty minutes earlier. While they were talking, the crowd in the pub had swollen and Alice had drawn in closer to his side. She was drinking fast, getting through her glasses of Pinot Grigio before Ned finished his pints, and he realised with surprise that she was feeling nervous. Every so often she would diffidently brush the hair from her brow behind her ear, only for it to fall back down again almost instantly.

'I saw from Facebook that Grace is in Chile,' Alice said.

'Ah, right, I didn't know that.' It wasn't a topic of conversation Ned would have chosen, and he didn't really want the image of his ex-girlfriend hanging over them while he talked to Alice, but after all, Grace was their only mutual friend, and perhaps the mention of her floated the sense of Ned's eligibility, boyfriend-worthiness, into the conversation. He liked the tone of intimacy and shared understanding with which Alice had broached it, cutting Piotr off on the far corner of the triangle. Ned wasn't Facebook friends with Grace anymore, now he thought of it, and he'd hardly been on the site in weeks except to add Alice after they'd met at the gym, and of course to look through her photo albums (oh, the green bikini pictures from the Maui trip . . .). 'She's dating a Chilean guy,' Ned said. 'Federico.'

'Yes, that's what it looked like.'

'I saw them a few months ago. He seemed like a nice guy.'

Alice gave Ned a mischievous look. 'But not a guy who could lift his own body weight, right?'

Ned grinned, and Alice – was he seeing this right? – winked at him slyly.

Piotr finished his third pint, and asked if Ned wanted to go to the Barber's Arms. As if he had remembered a point of etiquette, he then asked Alice too, only for her to look Ned brightly in the eye and say, 'What do you think?'

So Alice was assuming that she and Ned were going the same way. Excitement went through him like a bolt. 'I think we might have another one here,' he said, pretending to be casual.

Piotr started putting on his coat, mugging annoyance at being left out. He moved behind Alice's sight line, looked at Ned, nodded in her direction, then raised his thumb to his mouth and stuck his tongue into his cheek so it bulged out obscenely. Ned mouthed 'Fuck off' at him, and he did so, with a grin on his face.

'And then there were two,' Alice said. 'Maybe we should go somewhere quieter after these.'

Ned was amazed how the idea of their leaving together had formed in her mind without his even suggesting it. It all seemed natural and easy, the evening flowing in an inevitable direction.

'That sounds like a good idea,' he said, and drained the little bit of his pint that was left.

'I'm going to leave this actually,' she said, and placed

what was left of her wine on a nearby table. 'The wine is terrible. Shall we?'

They put their coats on, and as they left the bar, Ned heard someone behind him giving a camp wolf-whistle, followed by general laughter, which he took as acknowledgement that the hottest woman in the room was leaving on his arm. Alice was still wearing her high heels from the play, and lightly held his arm for balance. 'We could go to the Rochester,' she said, 'but it might be carnage on a Friday night.'

Ned decided to be bold. 'I have a bottle of wine at my place.'

'Where's that?'

'I'm just on Patmore Road,' he said. The name didn't seem to register with her. 'Five minutes away.'

'Well, let's do that then.'

On saturday morning, after Ned and Alice woke up together for the first time, they had sex again, before he made scrambled eggs and coffee while she showered and dressed. She ate a few forkfuls of egg, mentioned that she would be away for a week from Monday, and left. And Ned was on his own again in the bedsit, which looked the same as ever and showed no sign of the amazing happenings of the previous twelve hours. Ned pottered around the neighbourhood with a hilarious sense that none of the people going about their Saturday morning could guess what thrillingly charged scenes were replaying in his head from last night. When he brought his fingers to his face in the check-out queue at the supermarket, the smell of Alice's pussy went through him with a jolt.

In the next week, her text messages to him were warm. The high point came when she sent him, unsolicited, a selfie where she was lying in a huge hotel bathtub with only bubbles covering her breasts, and puckering her lips at the camera. Ned was sitting at his desk at work when the text came through, and replied, 'Très jolie'. A minute later she sent another picture, with the message 'Glad you think so matey', in which she had sculpted a thick beard of bubbles and was gurning and jutting her jaw like a pirate. She still looked gorgeous.

When Alice came back to London, part of Ned worried that the news might make its way back to Grace, and that she would be hurt that Ned was involved with one of her friends. Ned had a feeling Alice would be discreet, though – it was something about the way she carried herself, with a privacy that was only discarded in rather calculated ways. Ned became aware of this the first time they went to SunFit together. They were working out in different areas of the gym, Alice on the cross-trainers and Ned on the free weights; between his sets, Ned would look over at her and he was amazed – he'd never noticed this before – at how often random strangers approached her and initiated conversation. It happened four or five times in the brief period when Ned was watching, not just with men who were clearly trying to hit on her, but also with a couple of women who seemed to Ned, out of earshot, to be either complimenting her or asking for something, maybe for advice or recommendations. Each time, Alice held a tight smile, not breaking stride on her machine, and managed to send the person away in some good-natured but tough way, refusing to be embarrassed that these people were seeing her sweaty, red-faced and in lycra.

When Ned had almost finished his sets and was sitting on the steps of the fire escape recovering from his close-grip chin-ups, Alice approached him from behind and placed her hand on his shoulder. He jumped in shock, then laughed at himself.

'You're very sweaty,' she said.

'Don't come near. I'll stink.'

'It makes you look more hunky. *Even* more hunky, I should say.'

Ned took the compliment in his stride and said, 'Are you all done?'

'Pretty much. But I was hoping you might show me a few exercises over here. I mean, they showed me at the induction but it always seems a bit intimidating when I come in on my own.'

'I'd love to. Yeah, it can be a bit of a bear-pit here when the proper powerlifting guys are in.'

'The grunters, we call them.'

'Who's "we"?'

'We is *women*, Ned.' He laughed, and she cuffed the top of his head playfully. 'I've always wanted to try weight-lifting. I read a blog once about all the reasons why women should lift.'

Ned guided Alice through benchpresses, bent-over rows, military presses, squats and deadlifts. She was a natural, maintaining good form without even needing to be told that here she should keep her core tense or here she should arch her lower back or engage her glutes. Ned found it intensely sexy, to witness her instinctive physical grace, her sense of how the body could be plied.

While Ned stood over her head, spotting her bench-presses, he felt another hand press on his shoulder.

'Hey, man. You're gonna have me out of a job here.'

Ned turned to embrace him and said, 'Alice, this is my man, Darus.'

'Oh, we know each other already. How you doing, Alice?'

'I'm good. How are you?'

'Terrific. But listen, what are you doing training with this guy? If you wanted a trainer you should've come to me, I made this guy everything he is.'

'I didn't think you'd be able to handle me, Darus,' Alice said, and all three of them laughed.

'Best man fucking wins again,' Darus said, and slapped Ned on the back, before going off to meet a client.

Ten minutes later, while Ned waited at reception for Alice to get out of the changing room, Darus darted over from the gym floor to say, 'Dude, are you banging her?'

Ned stared at him and said, 'What do you think?'

'Well, I just want to say that you're a fucking legend.

I've been wanting to nail that chick for two years and got nowhere,' Darus said, pausing when Alice appeared around the corner, as if she knew they'd been talking about her, and shooed him away with a brisk wave of the hand.

As Ned spent more time with her over the next weeks – the same period in which he was developing his sockpuppets on Roidsweb – he found her way of being herself in the world more and more impressive. It must have come from her sense of being somewhat famous, he thought, having been an object of envies and desires that she had to keep at bay almost since childhood. Ned thought he could sense in her the remnants of several past selves: the high-achieving schoolgirl, with hints of brisk prefect and lacrosse captain; the girl who learned young that she was considered beautiful, and that this would inflect her relations with everyone she met, boys and girls and men and women alike, and was something she had to handle; the young woman to whom all doors were open but who didn't really know what she wanted much of the time, and didn't want to have to think about it. She didn't want the responsibility of being Alice Williams, in whom so many people's ideas were invested. When Ned came to understand this, he tried to treat her with as few expectations as possible, to check the impulse to project his fantasies onto her, and this seemed to suit her. When she came to his bedsit she would have her hair pulled back into a ponytail under a baseball cap, wearing a sloppy sweatshirt and jeans with no make-up, and if anything Ned found her more delightful in this freckle-nosed mode.

He found her openness lovely, and was moved by how readily she cried in front of him. The first time it happened, they were on the sofa in Alice's flat, Ned sitting upright and Alice lying with her head on his thigh while they watched TV, when he noticed the run of tears pulsing across her cheek and pooling in her ear. He asked what it was and she said, laughing at herself, 'Oh, it's just this woman's situation' (they were watching a programme about makeovers) – 'but don't worry, I basically like to have a good weep at least once a day.' Ned couldn't remember the last time he had cried in front of somebody else. It was usually a corny film in a dark cinema, rather than anything in his own life, that brought him to tears, and that only happened rarely. He had the feeling that Alice's openness was something he needed in his life.

Still, she sometimes took Ned aback when she casually mentioned things from her extraordinary life; when they were idly talking about relationships, she told him about a 'post-break-up fling' she'd had a few years ago with a British actor who now starred in Hollywood movies (apparently he was obsessively neat and tidy, and had a thin dick – Ned thought of it every time he saw his face on posters in underground stations). But then again, why should it be strange to Ned that he was dating a girl who'd had a fling with a famous actor?

It was in their fucking that Ned felt he saw Alice, and was seen by her, most clearly. It became more engrossing and exciting as they became more used to each other. It was a wonder to Ned, how Alice wanted him to be unembarrassed and unapologetic about naming his desires and satisfying them with her body. He saw now that it was unfair of him to hold resentments towards his ex-girlfriends for not being in tune with his desires, because really the fault was in him: he had been too inhibited to say what he wanted; he did it in a nervous, shame-shadowed way – *I mean, I wouldn't do anything you wouldn't want to, but . . .* – and this made his partners less likely to want to please him. Instead, with Alice, unflinchingly Ned would say that he wanted her to lick the head of his cock and squeeze his balls while he wanked himself off onto her tongue, or that he wanted to fuck her arse while they lay on their sides spooning and she used her vibrator, or she would tell him that she wanted him to lie next to her and rub around her clit in circles with two fingers while gently biting her nipples. And sometimes the other person would want to, and sometimes not; either way, the honesty of it, the sense that sex was simply something they could do with their bodies to please each other and themselves, turned Ned on immensely.

NED'S AIM WAS TO have 150 sockpuppet identities up and running on Roidsweb, each with a significant forum history and high kudos, based on the number of up-ratings their forum contributions had received, before his supplier site went live; 150 would be enough to make his site look reliable and encourage real forum members to order from him. If Ned was going to fabricate a customer base, he needed time to let it bed in and flourish. He had to stagger the creation of his user accounts; the turnover of members on the forum seemed busy enough that 150 new members spread over six weeks wouldn't seem especially irregular. A browser plug-in enabled him to set up an unlimited number of proxy servers located anywhere in the world; if anybody checked the IP addresses of his accounts, they would seem to be posting to the forums from across the UK, Europe, America and Australia.

Before he began creating his identities, Ned made a close study of the way people posted and interacted on Roidsweb, and of Piotr's tweets and articles as XTRMNTR. Ned liked Piotr's tone: even though some of his arguments about feminism and 'cultural Marxism' went a bit far, the writing was always lively, contentious and funny. Ned could see why Piotr had such a following. If Ned's own characters were going to be believable to other people, he had to believe in them himself, and to know as much about them as he could: their given names, the online handles they used, and what their choice of handle said about them; their age, race, sexual orientation and marital status; their bodybuilding expertise and past experience with steroids; their political inclinations, employment history and class background; how rich they were; the extent of their education; their tastes and sense of humour. He had to bear in mind continuity details: what time zone they were in, when they would be likely to post, what season it was, what the local idioms were. Most of all, he needed to know their motivation. Why did they get into bodybuilding? Why did they use gear? What was it that the Roidsweb community gave them?

As soon as he started, Ned found the work to be the most absorbing thing he had ever done. He approached it methodically. His workload at the office was fairly light at the moment, and recently he had been able to finish his tasks quicker than Piotr expected, but now, instead of spending the free hours looking at social media like the others in the office, he worked on his sockpuppets, with a decoy browser window ready to pop up and hide what he was doing at a moment's notice. The risk of being discovered wasn't very high; half the people in the office were sitting there looking at Facebook, and Roidsweb had a 'work mode' setting that removed the graphics from the top of the page and blocked images unless you specifically clicked to expand them. If anyone snooped, Ned could be on a web developer's forum for all they knew.

In the last month, word had gone round the office that redundancies were looking inevitable. Chevron had lost three major clients in six months. Piotr had been called in to two crisis meetings with the owners, and each time he came back to his desk he was quiet for the rest of the afternoon. Robin said they were being undercut by shell companies that outsourced design and programming to India, but Piotr said they couldn't know that for sure – and anyway, if Indian programmers were willing to work as hard as them for a quarter of the money, good luck to them.

The prospect of redundancies made some people anxious but seemed to liberate others into a giddy mood of distraction; regularly now the office, which was entirely staffed by men, was taken over by a game of indoor cricket or hacky-sack or by someone shouting out 'Three-minute mosh!' when a certain song came on the radio, at which everybody jumped up and did headbanging for the duration. Ned found this tiresome, and his reluctance to take part had been noted by some of his colleagues. After last week's Thursday hype session – an initiative Piotr had recently started, which involved spending the first fifteen minutes of the day in the meeting room doing team-building exercises, playing charades, or being made to sing songs or tell jokes to the rest of the group – Piotr had taken him aside and mentioned that his colleagues thought Ned wasn't really committing to the process, even though he had won the alphabet game with the category 'Capital Cities'. Ned thought Piotr had been strange with him ever since the evening he got together with Alice, anyway. Something had changed between them that night at *Doctor Faustus*.

Ned hadn't taken any holiday yet this year, and had an unused week carried forward from last year. He decided to take it all now in one go, starting in the first week of June, to give himself an unbroken stretch free for working on the project. He had an urge to get away from his regular, daily life, and set up conditions in which he could work with total concentration, even if it meant not seeing Alice for a little while. A bootcamp. He needed to hunker down for the next phase.

THE GALLERY OF BACK-TO-SCHOOL photos, the boy in them growing older as he climbed the wall of the stairs, abruptly cut off in the early teens when he refused to pose for the pictures anymore; the squadron of Airfix models hanging by threads from the bedroom ceiling and casting menacing shadows across the walls; the several seasons' worth of matchday programmes neatly ordered in binders gold-embossed with the club logo; the small libraries of fantasy novels, books on ancient Rome or *The X-Files*, enthusiasms that burned themselves out as quickly as they had flared up; the armies of lizardmen, chaos dwarfs and wood elves tucked up in shoeboxes – all the dead loves and humiliations of Ned's boyhood and youth sprang back into life when he returned to his old bedroom in the family home.

His belongings were exactly as he had left them, but in the years since he had moved away, his parents' things had started to encroach – boxfiles, knitting projects, reams of old printer paper – so that the room was now an office installed on top of a teenager's bedroom. To set up his laptop, Ned had to spend five minutes moving things aside before he could see the surface of the desk, growing more and more frustrated as he went, so that when his mum called up the stairs, 'Would you like a cup of tea and a piece of cake, Edmund?' he snapped back at her, 'I'm trying to work, mum!' before sheepishly adding, 'But, yeah, thanks, I would, I can come down and get it . . .'

The house felt cramped. Ned immediately regretted having taken the train there instead of renting a car; he wasn't insured on his parents' car, and would have to ask for a lift if he wanted to go anywhere. He felt like he could sense his parents tiptoeing around him and each other, hovering in the hallway outside his bedroom door. No matter: he had to shut it out and focus on his work.

On the Saturday, his first evening back at his parents' house, Ned created a character who lived in Gravesend in Kent, was 30 years old, and had the username *Florin Raducioiu*, after a footballer of the mid-90s. He worked in an insurance office. He had been a serious lifter for four years and went to the gym five times a week, rising at six to go before work. He lived with his girlfriend Danielle, who liked his physique but didn't know he was on gear. He was currently off-cycle but was planning his next stack for the early summer, to get bulked up before a beach holiday. The second, third and fourth sockpuppets Ned created that night had the usernames *Dr Van Deusen*, *joey deacon* and *bitches ain't shit*; they were all white English men, aged 38, 36 and 25. *joey deacon* was a hyper-aggressive, sarcastic Londoner who would often boast of his physical and sexual prowess; he had a girlfriend called Jade who was a glamour model, he had made a lot of money running a building firm, and he had been working out since he was a teenager.

Ned chose the username *live fast die young* for a character he called Tom Young, who lived in Tempe, Arizona, and sold second-hand books on Amazon, and the name *¡fullcommunism!* for a character called Luke Spree, who lived in London and worked as a sports journalist with a strong interest in left-wing politics. Luke Spree was a real person, whom Ned had known at university, and who went around campus with a preening superiority, forcing leaflets about world trade issues on people. It amused Ned very much to imagine him having taken up weightlifting and posting under the name *¡fullcommunism!* on a steroid forum.

To help him come up with the names, Ned used a name generator website where he entered the national origin, age and sex of the character, and it instantly generated as many names as he wanted. When he wanted an African-American man in his thirties, he was offered five outlandish beauties straight away: Kaden Strickland, Javin Atkins, Konner Sandoval, Maddix Dorsey and Blayze Knight. Ned was a bit sceptical, but guessed the names on the website's database must have some basis in fact. These names became some of his sockpuppets. Kaden Strickland, he decided, was 34, lived in New Jersey and worked in financial services. His user name on the forums was *Kaden*. He was highly competitive, liked to work hard and play hard, and was a long-term bodybuilder. He believed in small government and individual liberties but he didn't trust Republicans, who were just protecting the interests of rich white people as far as he was concerned; he voted for Ron Paul for President in 2008. He worked out five times a week, usually in the mornings before work, doing a back day, a chest day, a legs day, an arms day and a shoulders day. He didn't believe in cardio. He was a serious character, with firm moral principles and no noticeable sense of humour. He was keen to help his fellow roiders, but only if they helped themselves. If forum members showed that they hadn't done their homework before asking a question, *Kaden* came down hard on them.

Konner Sandoval, on the other hand, was a joker and a ladies' man who had been a heavy drug user during his days as a session musician, but gave that up in his mid-thirties and got into clean living. He wasn't really a serious bodybuilder, but liked the boost that an occasional cycle gave to his physique, and the attention it got him from women. Currently he was deputy manager of a cocktail bar in North

Carolina. Konner's user name, Ned decided, was *Kontract Killer*.

After every fifty minutes creating content for the forums, Ned took a ten-minute break during which he completed 100 press-ups, 100 abdominal crunches and forty chin-ups, dangling from the portable chin-up bar he had hung in the doorframe, with his knees bent up behind him. His dad watched him from the end of the corridor, and once gamely hung from the bar in his cardigan for a second, before groaning and aborting the attempt. Ned told him he just needed to build up to it by joining a gym and using the machine with the counter-weight for assisted pull-ups, but his dad said, 'Oh no, I'm really not the type for a gym, I don't know where you get it from' – and looked at Ned with puzzlement. Ned let the matter drop.

The work he was doing made him feel like an artist. He was surprised by his imaginative reach, the authenticity of detail that gave his identities the ring of truth. He had brought all of these characters into being, and every day that he worked on them, barricaded upstairs in his bedroom, fuelled by cups of tea brought by his mum, they were becoming deeper and more nuanced. They were taking on lives of their own.

UNDER THE USER NAME *Science Boy* – real name Oliver Clifton, age 26, from Cheshire – Ned started a new thread with the title 'Why the bloke with the big package?', and wrote:

> So why is it, every gym I go to (I travel a lot for work, so I use a lot of gyms as guest member), there's always THAT GUY. You know the one I mean. The one that's hung like a horse in the changing room, lying there naked in the sauna with his dong flopping over the side of the bench like a fireman's hose. And then why is it always THAT GUY who's the one who wants to talk to you while you're changing or drying off or just doing your thing. Like, he looks at you full-on, with his massive dong there looking up at you too. Come on, man, no one wants to see that. Okay yeah maybe I'm a bit jealous, maybe I don't have so much to show in that area but I make up for it with character! Am I the only one this happens to?

He left it thirty seconds, went to the window where he was logged in as *Amsterdam Arnie* and wrote:

> Man, I'm so sorry! Wasn't trying to hurt your feelings I just wanted to chat about how your work-out went. I'll try to be more aware next time and leave the snake in the cage. :)

Amsterdam Arnie's post received fifteen up-ratings within a couple of minutes, and soon other forum members were contributing to the thread to say 'That was awesome!!! Lol' or 'OMFG I was not expecting this topic to start up here' or 'never happened to me bro but good luck with that'. As *Paul Cicero* from Melbourne, Ned wrote:

> Couldn't sleep tonight but this is the funniest thing I've seen all week. Just to tell you Science Boy don't worry, my old lady tells me that "hung like a horse" is no fun at all, there's definitely such a thing as "too big" but no such thing as "too small" as long as you're a grower and have other skills. Me I'm somewhere in the middle.

To this, writing as *Castle Grayskull,* Ned replied:

> no such thing as "too small" lmfao have you never heard of a "micropenis"? google image search that shit if you want

to pee your pants laughing. or maybe science boy can show us a pic of his?

The discussion thread was on to the fourth page within an hour, with more than 100 replies, about a quarter of which were written by Ned. A consensus was building that it was one of the funniest threads ever on the forum.

'WHAT EXACTLY IS THE project you're working on up there?'

Ned turned from the TV to face his mum, who sat next to him on the sofa in the front room. He had been at his parents' house for four days. He bit off the corner of sandwich he had just dipped in his soup, put the rest of it back on the plate on his lap, and considered how to answer while he chewed.

'It's a bit hard to explain really. It's just a really big coding job, you know? It's for a website with a very complicated back end and lots of dynamic content on the front end that needs to be responsive on all different devices.'

'It all sounds very technical,' she said. Ned nodded and looked back to the dancing programme, glad to have headed off any follow-up questions, but his mother said, 'We just think you might be working a bit too hard, Edmund. You know how you can get obsessive about things. It's good that you're doing your exercises up there, we can hear you doing that, but I just wonder if you ought to be going outside more. You were up there all day today, on a lovely June day.'

Ned looked at her irritably. 'Do you think I should go to the rec and throw a stick around for myself to chase?'

'No, your mother's right, Neddy,' said his dad. 'Life's not just about pushing yourself and working hard and doing your press-ups and whatnot. It's about, you know, enjoying life too.'

Ned rolled his eyes. It was typical of them to try to undermine what he was doing like this. For the first time in his life he was managing to make something of himself, and they wanted to hold him back. Typical! How much did either of them 'enjoy' life? No, they were just scared of him thriving, he thought, because it would reveal to them their own failure to do so. It was the same the previous day when he had told them that the person he was always texting was his sort-of girlfriend, and that she was an actress. His mum had looked worried and said, 'Oh, but it's terribly difficult to make a living as an actress, you know' – as if it was a career she herself had considered and wisely thought better of. Something in Ned sank at the defeatism and smallness of the life he had grown up with – the fearfulness, the inviting of failure, the minuscule treats doled out with pathetic caution and barely enjoyed . . . He felt the impulse to tell his mother that no, actually, Alice didn't have any trouble at all making a living and didn't even worry about it, that she liked to randomly go out for four rounds of champagne cocktails on a weeknight and then take a black cab home . . .

But his frustration dissipated into a painful sympathy for his parents, for the little worries and barely submerged insecurities that had hardened into fixed, unchangeable character. In the past he had felt the weight of their fear of life to be suffocating, but now . . . things were different somehow. He had to let them be themselves, Philip and Rosemary, a quantity surveyor and a district nurse, both nearing retirement, pottering along and doing the best they could, in their way. They weren't going to change now. Ned wanted to reach out to them, but he also knew he had to keep them at bay, to keep a buffer zone between the version of himself he could be in this house, caught within limits set out when he was a teenager, and the real life he was leading now.

'I do enjoy my life,' he said. 'I think I've never been happier. It's just that I have to throw myself into this project at the moment, because really good things could come of it.'

ALONG WITH HIS MALE-BORN sockpuppets, Ned created an account with the username *Trans Guy*, for a character with the offline name Daniel Marsh. Daniel Marsh had been christened Rachel Marsh and was in the process of transitioning. He worked as a photographer in Vermont, struggling to pay the rent, so he didn't have health insurance; being unable to get a testosterone prescription from a doctor, he had decided to go the DIY route. He thought of himself as a gender hacker. Starting on testosterone was the first step in a journey the end of which was unknown to him, but he definitely wanted to have top surgery as soon as he could. He was trying to save some money each month to go to Mexico and have the operation there. For now though, he was loving the new feeling of strength he had on gear, the way his muscles were becoming heavier and the fat was dropping away from his hips, and the way the dark hairs were spreading more thickly on his forearms, extending up from his bush towards his belly button, and sprouting on his cheeks, chin and neck. He loved how horny he felt, as if his clitoris were transforming into a permanently erect cock before his eyes. His girlfriend, Beatrice, was supporting him through his transition. They had been together since the time when he was still known as Rachel. At first, she had been afraid of his starting on testosterone: What if he got roid rage, she thought, or died of a heart attack at forty-five? But Daniel calmed her worries. After extensive research, he prepared a dossier of information on the use of testosterone in F2M transitions for Beatrice to read. Together they met with some trans men who had gone through the same process at a local gender support clinic. One of the men they met, Gregg, had gone all the way to having bottom surgery, and cheerfully showed them his surgically constructed penis, made from tissue grafts from his forearms and skin from his backside. Daniel was impressed, though he doubted he would want to go through that himself. It was only his breasts he felt really dysmorphic about. He was binding them tight every morning, sometimes leaving himself short of breath from the constriction of his lungs. When he took off his binder before bed, Beatrice would massage the deep red impressions the elastic had made in the skin of his back and sides. Ned became so involved in creating the character that he seriously considered starting a blog for Daniel where he would document his life and the process of transition.

On the forums, *Trans Guy* was a calm, generous, humorous

presence, and in general, other posters treated him with respect. Once Ned made *Roider of the Lost Ark* write on the thread that *Trans Guy* had started about his transition, 'Nothing against trannies but it sounds like you're not a patch on a Thai ladyboy', and Ned was touched to see how many other forum members – genuine ones, not accounts run by him – waded in to defend *Trans Guy*. Lots of them also down-voted *Roider of the Lost Ark*'s post, which did some damage to his kudos, but when Ned had him make an apology for his comment, which was intended as a joke but which, he admitted, was ignorant and offensive, his kudos recovered. The gains in *Trans Guy*'s reputation, caused by the flood of sympathetic posts and up-voting, made it worthwhile. Ned went downstairs to have dinner with his parents, feeling satisfied with his evening's work.

‘I’M GETTING A BIT worried that my period is so late. You don’t think I’m pregs, do you?’

Ned texted back to ask exactly how late it was, and Alice said three days, though the app she used to track it could be slightly out. Ned said that he thought it was very unlikely – they’d been quite careful – and she shouldn’t worry. Then he set to thinking about it properly. They hadn’t been using condoms, but Ned hadn’t come in her pussy, he was pretty sure (although might it still have been on his hands that time?) . . . The thought submerged under these was whether he was even capable of getting someone pregnant right now. It wasn’t so long ago that he was in shutdown during his cycle, at which point there probably weren’t any sperm in his come at all; from what he’d read on the topic, it could take up to six months for fertility to return to full capacity after a cycle, even though natural testosterone production could be back up within a few weeks. If Alice was pregnant, might it not even be his? They hadn’t said that they were seeing each other exclusively; it had only been a few weeks, after all . . . The whole question pressed on his mind anxiously. He could hardly work out what he really thought about it. He sent Alice another message saying that it was definitely impossible, put the matter out of his mind and set to work.

It was Wednesday, his fifth day with his parents. His creations were bedding in nicely. Their kudos was building. Their relationships with other forum members were becoming more real. Many of them were now crucial voices on the forum. *Roider of the Lost Ark* tended to take the same positions as *Kaden* in forum discussions, and to back him up; *joey deacon* would often undercut them with a piss-taking remark, but he broadly respected their knowledge of lifting and gear; *Castle Greyskull* would wade in after *joey deacon* in a way which sometimes looked too friendly, as if he was trying to gain favour with him. *Pemulis* would always bring everything back to porn stars, and *Gundog* would egg him on. *Gary Glitter* would write wry accounts of things that happened in the gym and in his day-to-day life, and most of Ned's other users would respond positively to them; sometimes *Mr_MXYZPTLK* would write on a thread, 'i think this calls for a glitterizing', and *Gary Glitter* would give his own comic take on the discussion. *Chevvy Chevalier* would comment on everybody's training logs, pushing them to raise their lifts. *Exomonster* would do the same, but whereas *Chevvy Chevalier*'s lifts were modest, since he was six foot eight and naturally very skinny, *Exomonster*'s lifts were huge, approaching competition levels, but he would discuss them with an endearing modesty. This modesty generally brought him the respect of Ned's other sockpuppets, though some, including *Kaden*, regarded his claims with suspicion. Once *Kaden* challenged his claim to be benching 240 kg by saying 'pics or it didn't happen', only for *Exomonster* to say 'LOL you think I'm going to post personal pics that might identify me on a steroid site?'

Ned was in his stride, adding more new users at intervals every day. He had a series of A4 hardback notebooks in which he kept details of their back-stories, personal histories and major posts, and pretty soon each of them had a rich, textured existence in his mind. Sometimes he would pace back and forth, speaking in their voices, playing out conversations between them, standing by the sink in the corner to watch himself in the mirror as he impersonated them, and cackling at his own invention. Once, his dad surprised him by knocking on the bedroom door and backing his way in with a mug of tea when Ned hadn't heard him coming up the stairs. He found Ned flushed and giddy after scrambling to minimise his browser windows. Ned felt the urge to shout at him, feeling caught out, but he let the beat drop and the moment passed. 'Were you on the phone to someone?' his dad asked, and he told him smirkingly no, he'd been talking to himself. His dad looked at him with cautious amusement – 'Righto, Neddy' – and placed the mug down.

He was so absorbed in the details of the rich world he had created that the atmosphere of the real world became strange to him, as if something had gone out of it. It was as if the people going about their business in his hometown were pretending, putting on a show for his benefit, and when he turned away from them and went back to the world of his sockpuppets, they would give up the act, barely remembering what the point of it had been in the first place.

After six hours of solid work, Ned remembered that his phone had buzzed a few minutes ago to say he had a message. He took it from his pocket to find a photograph sent by Alice showing a troop of old-style British soldiers, with cocked hats, long coat-tails, and muskets slung over their shoulders, trotting in formation across a field absurdly.

'Eh?' he wrote.

Twenty seconds later, Alice's reply: 'It means: The redcoats are coming! Panic over ;)'

Ned's shoulders dropped and he felt a tension, present for so long at the back of his neck that he'd ceased to notice, instantly disperse. Then he checked his work email and found a message from Piotr asking him to come in for a meeting at nine fifteen the next morning.

'YOU MIGHT PROBABLY BE able to guess why I've asked you in. I know there's been a lot of uncertainty recently in the office, so I hope it'll be good to make all of that less, you know, uncertain.'

Piotr seemed nervous. When Ned had found his message the previous afternoon, he replied, 'Am in the sticks at my parents' place, but sure. See you then' – and had jokingly added, 'Hope I'm not in trouble :)' – only for Piotr to reply, 'Please just come in at 9:15', with no hint of the banter he would normally have come up with in an email to Ned. Ned knew immediately that he was going to be offered redundancy. Why else would Piotr have called him in when he was on leave?

It was something of a surprise. He thought that if they were going to lay off one senior developer it would be Robin, who surely earned more than Ned, having been there longer, and wasn't as good as him at coding. But then again, the owners of the company were unpredictable, and if he thought about it, Ned probably had been giving off a sense of dissatisfaction in the job recently. He'd hardly been to the pub with the others for weeks before going on leave . . . Ned finished his afternoon's work on the forums, packed the clothes that were strewn across his bedroom back into his travel bag, told his parents he was heading back to London, and caught the train, sent on his way with a roast chicken sandwich that his mum made him for the journey.

'I can guess what "uncertainty" means, Piotr,' Ned said. 'You're going to tell me that you want to lay me off?'

'If we're being blunt, then yes.' Piotr seemed almost relieved to have the unpleasant business taken out of his hands. He smiled, stretched back in the chair and rolled his shoulders.

'Can I ask how many redundancies there are going to be?'

'I can't discuss other people's situations, Ned –'

'For fuck's sake, Piotr, it's me you're talking to.'

'Okay, let me tell you then. We're streamlining the roles of one senior web development position and one junior.'

' "Streamlining". So that's me and Will then?'

Piotr made a small motion of the head, less than a nod, to indicate that Ned wasn't wrong. Ned had thought two of the five full-timers were going to be laid off, and that it was unlikely he'd be one of them. Now it turned out he was the only one of the five. It didn't add up.

'Can I ask what the rationale is for choosing me? Because

it seems to me that based on my skills and my recent performance, I'm at least one of the two highest calibre members of the team.'

Piotr interlinked his fingers in his lap, immediately raised his arms to cross them in front of his chest, and looked off to a point on the wall behind Ned's head. 'It's true that at management level everyone's broadly satisfied with your performance. There are other issues to do with your wider professionalism.'

'Like what?'

Piotr wouldn't meet Ned's eye.

'There have been concerns raised about your use of illegal drugs, for example—'

'Oh, for fuck's sake, Piotr—'

'It's true, I am not the only one to have raised it, and you have confirmed the allegation to me personally. The problem is that this open use of, umm, steroid drugs raises problems for the image and the professional relations of the company. What do you think our clients think when they meet a webdev who is so . . .' – Piotr couldn't find the word but substituted for it a mime of puffing out his cheeks and spreading his shoulders.

'That's fucking garbage, Piotr. How many times have I seen you and Robin go off to the loos at the pub to do lines of coke together? I've seen you do it with my own eyes.'

Piotr said nothing and slid a stapled document across his desk towards Ned.

'Is this my redundancy offer then?'

'Yes. Since you've been working here for six years, you are entitled to the statutory offer of a week's salary for each year of service, so the sum is six weeks' salary.'

Ned almost broke out laughing. Six weeks! All the talk in the office had been about how generous the redundancy packages were going to be – Robin had heard a rumour that they were prepared to go up to four times the statutory amount, although most of the others thought that three times was more likely. Now it was clear to Ned why he had been chosen: they thought they could get away with using this 'drugs' bullshit as a pretext for offering him the smallest possible pay-off. Ned looked at Piotr, without saying anything, for half a minute, and finally said, 'I don't intend to accept your offer.'

'If I were you,' Piotr said, 'I would keep in mind that these concerns about professional conduct could also be grounds for dismissal, if the company wanted to pursue that option.'

'I don't intend to accept the offer,' Ned said, before getting up from his chair and leaving the office.

ALICE HAD STAYED OVER at Ned's bedsit the previous night. He'd texted her when he decided to come back to London for the meeting, and three hours later there she was, sitting in the burrito shop looking at her phone while she waited for him. A throb seemed to move through him when he saw her; there was something almost wondrous in re-encountering the intensity of her presence, her fierce separateness, as she sat there simply getting on with her life, as she'd been doing all the time he was away. Maybe, he thought, it meant that he was in love with her. Alice! She looked up, as if she had heard his thoughts, saw him, and waved.

On the bus home from the office after his meeting with Piotr, Ned had wondered if Alice would still be in his bed when he got back, and fantasised vaguely about joining her there. But when he came in, she was dressed and sitting straight-backed on the bed's edge. Ned leaned in to kiss her on the cheek but she kept her head still and her eyes cast down.

'Are you going to rehearsals?' he said.

'There's something we need to talk about.'

‘Oh yes?’ Ned said. He was still pottering around the room, taking his keys, wallet, change and phone from his trouser pockets and putting them in their places. ‘I hope I’m not in trouble,’ he said, and sniggered to himself.

‘Are you on steroids?’

This was too much. On the same day as Piotr! Ned turned back towards her and said in a thin voice, with all the colour gone out of it, ‘Why do you ask that?’

‘I found all your syringes and needles and shit.’

‘Why were you looking through my stuff? I leave you alone in my place and you start going through my stuff? That box was locked for a reason.’

‘You left the key in the lock.’

Ned felt sick in his belly, as if he suddenly needed the toilet. ‘Why were you poking around under my bed anyway?’

‘Is that really the point? If you have to know, I dropped one of my rings when I was getting dressed and it rolled under there.’

‘Right,’ said Ned. ‘Right. Well that’s just perfect.’

‘You haven’t answered my question.’

‘The answer is no, I’m not currently on steroids.’

Alice gripped Ned by the wrist with surprising strength. ‘What do you mean, “currently”?’

‘I did one cycle earlier this year, but I’m currently off-cycle.’

‘ “Off-cycle”? Ned . . . what the fuck?’

‘Since when did you become anti-drugs?’

‘You know I’m not anti-drugs in general but, Jesus, *steroids*? I mean, seriously? Are you trying to become a nightclub bouncer?’

‘Look, you’ve got the wrong idea about this. It’s not like that at all. It’s just a way of improving on your natural capabilities. Think of it like that.’

‘You’re saying taking steroids is *natural*? Jesus-fucking-hell, that’s a good one.’

‘No, I didn’t mean that. I don’t give a fuck what’s natural. Come on, it’s not exactly natural when you take MDMA with your actor friends every weekend, is it?’

‘I don’t know why you say “actor friends” like that. Yes, we’re actors, but that’s not as weird as having a secret junkie stash that no one else knows you’re shooting up. Were you planning on ever telling me?’

Ned didn’t know the answer to that. ‘I didn’t know whether you’d understand. Clearly not, it seems.’

‘What the fuck is there to understand? That the guy I’m dating is a WWF wrestler who’s going to flip out and murder me?’

‘Roid rage is garbage, for one thing. A total myth.’

‘Oh for fuck’s sake, Ned.’

‘Look, I can explain it. It started when Darus recommended

it to me, and I was sceptical at the start just like you, I thought it was cheating, I thought it was for bodybuilding freaks, all that stuff. But he explained it to me – and he's a qualified, licensed personal trainer – and I read an enormous amount about it, and actually it's very safe, there are people with a huge amount of experience who you can learn from. It's just the same as the fancy male health clinics they advertise on those posters on the tube. No difference. And the truth is it's improved my life enormously. Transformed it. I can't believe I didn't discover it until I was thirty.'

'I don't know what to say, Ned, I find all this too weird. And the thing that upsets me is, I've seen this exact thing before: my first ever boyfriend, he was at Marlborough, and he started being all secretive and moody and the next thing I know he's in a rehab clinic for his heroin problem. And we were sixteen years old, for god's sake. So my feeling is, I just don't want to go through that again. It makes me want to run a mile, quite frankly.'

Ned had flipped open his Macbook and loaded up Roidsweb. He sat down on the bed beside Alice with the machine on his knees. 'Look. I honestly think that if you read a little bit about gear you'll see why it's totally different to that situation.'

Alice looked at the screen for a second then brought her gaze back to Ned's face. 'Ned, look at me. I'm not going to start reading some bodybuilding support group so you can convince me that steroids are a good thing. Are you serious?'

Ned said nothing. Alice stood and picked up her bag. She had packed all the things she had left at Ned's place over the last weeks, so that they bulged out of the top of the bag. 'I need time to think about this, Ned. Frankly it makes me very unsure whether we can carry on seeing each other,' she said, and made for the door.

When Alice had left, Ned opened his work email and found a message from Piotr, attaching the redundancy offer and reminding him that he needed to accept it before his leave ended in three weeks.

IF NED WANTED HIS website to look credible, he had to get the details right. He made a careful study of the design features of Amazon, Argos and the top steroid sources. Then he set about designing and building the site.

He decided to have log-in, shopping trolley and checkout buttons at the top of the screen, with a running total next to the trolley. The product categories ran in a column down the left-hand side of the screen, and this column remained in place on all sub-pages. For the colour scheme, he made a navy-blue background with light-blue detailing. At the bottom of the screen he placed stock images of smiling, trustworthy-looking doctors and nurses, next to the Terms and Conditions and FAQ buttons, which linked to disclaimers saying that no one should use these products without a prescription and medical supervision, that they were health products not intended for leisure use, and so on. When customers placed items in their shopping trolley and went to check out, they were taken to an online form which had been prepopulated with their order details, and all they had to do was fill in their delivery address and contact email and press send. The site logged all this in the database that Ned accessed through the control panel. There was a notice next to the form saying that the site only accepted orders that provided a securely encrypted email address, from Hushmail or a similar provider.

Ned had finished the basic architecture of the site. It was ready to go live whenever he had written the product descriptions and adequately prepared the ground with his sockpuppets. After brainstorming possible names, drawing up a longlist and checking which addresses were available, he purchased the domain name Gear4u.net.

3

GEAR4U WENT LIVE IN late June, six weeks from the day when Ned had started bedding in his sockpuppets. He had uploaded the product descriptions, proofread the website text, tested the order form and found that the order arrived safely in the database. He had acquired a driver's licence bearing his photograph and the name 'Brian Logan', and drafted an email about payment details, telling people to make out the Western Union cash transfer to Brian Logan at his local post office branch. Everything was ready.

Ned set up a supplier profile on Roidsweb for Gear4u and started a thread on the Supplier Introductions board:

> Hi Roidswebbers. Please check out gear4u.net, our new site. We're a young start-up offering top-quality, pharma-grade products in sports training, hormone and PCT categories along with a range of orals and peripherals. We're based in the UK but ship worldwide within 24 hours of receiving your payment and try to reply to all orders within 3 working hours. We're looking to take this to a serious and professional level so please feed back to us, rate

us and help us build the brand. For the first week all customers coming to the site from Roidsweb get a 15% discount – just enter the code "RW2012". We've really pushed the boat out to offer this discount, and stripped back our margin to the limit in order to offer you the best deal, so please do take advantage of this grand opening special offer!

Best wishes,

Kira,

gear4u.net customer service manager

Ned had decided to develop a female persona to deal with sales. He thought it would help to command respect from forum members if there was a woman reading and replying to their messages. It would look professional. He had witnessed how the more forthright forum members would interact aggressively with suppliers if there was any problem with an order – a hold-up in acknowledging receipt of money, a delay in delivery, a seizure at customs, or an underdosed vial – and he knew that things might get sticky in a few weeks' time.

He waited three minutes, changed to the window where *joey deacon* was logged in, and wrote, 'Nice site, very professional. Might try you out soon. Has anyone else ordered from this supplier?' As *Roider of the Lost Ark*, Ned wrote,

'Top marks for site design, maybe I'll try out a small order', and as soon as he had pressed 'post', he had another reply from *Mike Katz's T-Shirt* saying 'Good luck with the start-up. I need a new source after a few disappointments from my last supplier so I'll definitely try this out and report back.'

Ned posted customer reviews from eight of his sockpuppets in the two days after the site went live: *9goth*, *Leytonstone*, *joey deacon*, *Dr Van Deusen*, *Mr_MXYZPTLK*, *Flash*, *¡fullcommunism!*, and *craig david's diary*. All the reviews said more or less the same thing: that they were trying out this new supplier with a first-time order; that they were really impressed by the customer service and response time. For some, Ned said their gear had arrived already, discreetly and well packaged, with impressive speed, and they looked forward to pinning it; for others he waited another day before saying it had arrived, by which time he had posted another twenty customer reports. As *craig david's diary* wrote:

> It looks like Gear4u could be the answer to my prayers! I've been looking for a reliable UK-based source for months and so far they're totally on point: a smooth, clear order process, great comms, and super-fast delivery. I pinned my first shot yesterday and I'm buzzing about it already. Excellent work, Kira et al.

NED HAD CONFRONTED THE matter of his redundancy offer the week before the site went live. Once the initial surprise of Chevron's low offer had subsided, he didn't feel worried about the situation. If things went to plan, he should soon have enough cash to tide him over for a while, and he'd been wondering whether he should move on before Piotr called him in for the meeting anyway. Six years at the same agency was too long, everyone in the office had been annoying him recently, and the way his sense of himself had changed in the last months made him feel like he was ready for a greater challenge. Turning up every day to fiddle away with the code for other people's websites, laugh at Piotr's jokes, eat sweaty sandwiches at his desk and listen to shit music on the radio: why should he settle for that as a life? His weeks on leave had given him a sense of how much he could do with his time when he had it all to himself.

What he needed was some leverage in the negotiations. Six weeks' salary was a pathetic offer, and they thought they could get away with it by pinning this misconduct threat on him. It was a low tactic, after all the work he had given them. He had never caused a single problem, and had always been under-appreciated. He turned over potential responses to the offer in his mind for several days, and got as far as drafting some cutting phrases he could use in an email. But he knew that wasn't enough. He needed to come back at them with something as ruthless as their offer.

Ned was in the gym, feeling pumped after a huge drop-set of military presses with no rest between reps, when the answer came to him, fully formed and almost too perfect-seeming; he clapped his hands in glee at the thought and said, 'Ha!', so that the wiry old man doing bicep curls in the mirror looked at him suspiciously.

At home, the materials took less than an hour to prepare. The process of gathering them was highly amusing to him. When he was finished, he replied to Piotr's email with a short, courteous message that said he was declining the offer, and wanted to make a case for his receiving not one but four weeks' worth of salary for each year he had worked for the agency, on the grounds of his loyalty and good service. Then he created a new, anonymous Hushmail account, and composed a message to Piotr's personal address:

Piotr,

You will have received my official reply to your redundancy offer now. Consider this an unofficial extension of that reply. I want four weeks for each year of service (total: 24 weeks) plus the guarantee of a clean reference for future employers. If you do not accept these terms I will send to Alex, Fabian and other key figures in the industry, including all major B2B publications and websites, a twenty-five page document which confirms your authorship of all online posts under the name XTRMNTR, and which contains excerpts, screencaps and links to sexist and racist content such as the following:

[thread] Why does every girl have a rape story? (March 2011)
[article] The five reasons why you should never date a black girl (April 2011)
[article] Feminism, cultural Marxism and the 'rape culture' myth (June 2011)
[blogpost] Positive discrimination promotes mediocrity (October 2011)
[thread] sluts who send nude pics deserve to have them leaked (January 2012)

This document is already prepared. If I receive a satisfactory redundancy package offer within ten working days, the document will be deleted; if not, it will be forwarded to the people named earlier in this message on Monday 2nd July.

I await your response.

N

ALICE TEXTED NED TWO minutes after he pressed send on his email to Piotr: 'Am in the hood . . . can I come round? Ax'

To Ned, it felt fated: he had taken a bold step in his handling of the redundancy question, and now he was being rewarded for his boldness. Of course Alice wanted to see him again. He had avoided contacting her since their argument two weeks ago, judging that it was best not to apologise – after all, he still didn't believe he'd done anything wrong – but to leave her to make the move. In the meantime, he had thought about her often; he only needed to look up from his screen at the blank wall behind and allow his gaze to become unfocussed, to hear her voice and picture her body in the most intimate detail. And now here she was: twenty minutes after her text message, her voice appeared on the intercom and she materialised at his door, smelling of cigarettes and coconut shampoo. The intensity of her presence struck him afresh.

Things flowed easily: they kissed; they sat down on the

sofa, talked about nothing for a few minutes; Ned suggested that they go out for a late drink.

'Come here first,' Alice said, and led him by the hand over to the bed. She lay down on her side, Ned stretched out next to her, they kissed, and Ned ran his hands up and down her back through her shirt. Then she turned onto her back, undid her jeans, took Ned's right hand and guided it down. 'Do it over my knickers like that,' she said. In the final moments she was tensing so hard that her white-knuckle grip on his shoulder slipped and her left hand smashed him in the face, making Ned snort with pain and laughter while Alice shook and gasped.

Ned was slightly wary of going to the cocktail bar on the corner of his street, since he and Piotr had once been there together, and he didn't want to bump into him. But it was eleven o'clock on a Monday; he decided not to worry about it. Ned and Alice ordered two mojitos, went to the deserted downstairs room with red carpets and furnishings illuminated by red lightbulbs, and settled into a plushly leathered booth.

'How's work?' said Ned, chewing a mint leaf.

'Good, actually – I've got this big audition on Friday for a TV pilot, which looks like it could be very exciting.'

'Oh, excellent. What is it?'

'It's about estate agents in Tottenham after the riots. Oi, don't laugh!' She shoved at Ned's shoulder in mock annoyance.

'I didn't say anything. No, it sounds like a good idea. No one's ever made a drama about the property market, have they? I really hope you get it.'

'Me too.'

'I find it hard to see you as an estate agent though. All the ones I meet are twenty-year-old Asian lads with too much gel in their hair.'

'Well, it's lucky I'm such a fabulous actress then, isn't it?'

After he had brought down a second round of mojitos from the bar upstairs, Alice asked Ned about his work. He told her he was thinking of taking voluntary redundancy, and was negotiating the pay-off now. She asked what he would do and he said he might take a career break, or go and live somewhere else for a while. They discussed where Ned might go. Alice was in favour of Berlin, where she'd been earlier that year on a fashion shoot. Neukölln, she said – the friend she'd stayed with there had a huge studio flat, sixty square metres, and it cost her about five hundred euros a month or something. To pay for it, she only had to work a few days every month, or stay over at her boyfriend's and rent out her flat to tourists through a website. And if he went to live in Berlin, Alice said, she could come and stay with him whenever she wanted.

'I wasn't sure you'd want to see me again, after last time,' Ned said.

Alice looked down at her drink. 'I've come round to the idea. I mean, I'm not saying I'm crazy about you doing . . . what we talked about, but I spoke to my friend Matt – you met Matt, didn't you? – and he said he knew loads of people who've used steroids, models and actors and people like that. I was surprised, but it did make me think that you might not be *such* a weirdo. I just wish you'd told me about it and I didn't have to stumble on it myself, like it's some big secret.'

'I'm sorry about that,' Ned said.

'You're such a sillyhead sometimes. I just want you to tell me the truth.'

A pause. Ned felt the moment open up before him. Should he tell her, or not? Suddenly the urge became overwhelming, and it felt like the easiest thing in the world. Yes, he would tell her.

'There's another aspect to it, actually.'

'Oh yes?' said Alice brightly.

'This project I'm working on at the moment – it's actually a bit of a scheme related to that.'

Alice looked at him blankly.

'You remember I showed you that steroid forum when

we spoke about it – the one that all the companies use for selling their gear? Well, I've managed to get hold of quite a large stock at very low cost, and I'm basically building a website and a marketing operation to resell it to people at a profit. It could be quite a lot of money if it works. I'm launching it next Monday.'

Alice's eyes lit up. 'So that can fund Berlin. How exciting. Are you telling me you're becoming a drug dealer?'

'Well, it's prescription drugs,' Ned said, wondering briefly why he had been unable to tell her the whole truth about the fake gear, then letting the thought drop.

'I've always wanted to date a real badboy,' Alice said. She took a black cocktail napkin from the table, draped it across her head, pouted and said, 'Do you think I'd make a good gangster moll?'

'I didn't know they wore bonnets.'

'It's my pinstripe hat!'

They had finished their mojitos. While Ned fished for the mint leaves with his straw, Alice reached under the table, patted around his lap until she found his cock, still half-erect from earlier, and said, 'We should head back – we didn't do you yet, did we?'

GEAR4U RECEIVED ITS FIRST order on the second evening after going live. An email arrived from *Captain Vegetable*, who wanted two vials of Testosterone Cypionate and 200 tablets of Clomid, at a total of £140 once the 15% discount had been applied, plus the flat-rate £20 postage fee which Ned charged for each order. The postal address he had given for delivery was in Newcastle; his real name, or at least the name he wanted the parcel addressed to, was Dave Galvin. Ned sent the details for the Western Union transfer by email straight away, and within half an hour, *Captain Vegetable* emailed back to say he had made the transfer. Ned could hardly contain himself. It was real – at last it was real. He found himself still pacing his room, charged with excitement, twenty minutes later.

The post office was closed for the day, but by the time Ned went along with his ID to collect the cash at nine the next morning, he had received nine more legitimate orders, totalling more than £1,500. Five of the orders were from the UK, one was from the Netherlands, two were from Germany and one was from Greece. Six of these customers had already made their cash transfer, and four had left feedback on the excellence of Gear4u's customer service. While this was going on, Ned had created a further ten feedback reports. He had also started a thread as *Ill Phil*, entitled 'Why do your exes always seem sexier after you've broken up with them?' – a discussion which generated some lively points of view.

Summer was reaching its height. The sky was blue; the air was fresh. In the churchyard at the top of Ned's road, the roses were thrusting towards the air. He walked home from the post office with more than a thousand pounds in cash in his pocket and his head blazing with possibilities.

He decided on a system: he would visit the post office three times a day – once when it opened, once at lunchtime and once at closing time – and each time he would send off the parcels for which he had picked up the cash on his previous trip, and collect the cash from new orders. In between these visits, he would divide his time between packaging the orders, creating forum posts and supplier reviews from his sockpuppets, and responding to emails. He placed a 15% discount voucher for the customer's second order, rising to 25% if they spent more than £300, inside each jiffy bag, with a code that the customer had to quote in their next order to claim the discount. He hoped that the size of the discount would be enough to tempt people to place some large return orders.

When Ned returned to the bedsit after his lunchtime trip to the post office, he found an email from Piotr. The message said that Chevron was making Ned a new redundancy offer: for his final payment he would receive four weeks' wages for each of his six years of service. Twenty-four weeks' wages would give Ned a tax-free lump sum of just over £15,000. He accepted the offer straight away.

MORE ORDERS CAME. NED had been stuffing the cash he collected from the post office into a jiffy bag until Alice offered to sort through it for him and sat cross-legged on the bed, licking her thumb and dividing the notes into piles which she bound up with rubber bands. Ten minutes later she said, 'Done!', and Ned turned round from the desk to see her waving two neat little bundles of notes in each hand.

On the fifth day after the site had gone live, Ned decided it was time to moderate the universally positive feedback that Gear4u had received so far, just to keep things credible. He logged in under the user name *Bladen* and posted a complaint on the review page:

> I ordered test c, tren and deca from gear4u on Monday but they hav'nt replied yet. Very dissapointed about this after reading all the +ve fb on here the last few days.

Ned waited ten minutes, changed to the window where he was logged in from the official Gear4u account, and replied:

Dear Bladen: You failed to supply an encrypted email address. Please read the HOW TO ORDER section in the supplier introduction again. Customer security is a high priority for us and we therefore insist on a secure email contact. We endeavour always to reply within three working hours of receiving an order.

Regards,

Kira @ gear4u.net.

Then he waited five minutes, went back to the *Bladen* window, and replied to his own reply:

sorry sorry my mistake! thx for the promped response. have re-ordered now and can confirm email reply received already! great amazing service! can't wait 2 get my stash! #gymaddict #roidlust #madpumps #pumps

Ned shut the window, sat back, re-read the whole exchange, and read it aloud to Alice. She laughed. He was especially pleased with the spelling mistakes and with *Bladen*'s jumpy, exclamation-heavy style. How truly he had caught an authentic voice, and with what fineness of detail! In the time it had taken him to construct the exchange, he had received two more orders.

AN ORDER ARRIVED THROUGH the website on the Saturday of the first week for two vials of Test-Cyp, two vials of Trenbolone, a vial of Equipoise, two bottles of Nolvadex and two bottles of Clomid, for a total of £410. Clearly this was somebody stocking up for a major cycle. The delivery address: Darus Gaynesford at his flat in Stockwell.

It took a few seconds for the name to register. Ned hadn't seen Darus in three weeks. Of course, it made sense; it was Darus who had told Ned about Roidsweb in the first place, so it was only natural that he used the site himself. But somehow Ned had buried this information. He had probably been interacting with Darus on the forums without even knowing it. He tried to guess which username Darus might be, and was baffled for a few minutes, before it came to him: Darus must be *BeastMode84*, who occasionally posted in threads about politics, sports and relationships. It was *BeastMode84*'s frequent references to *The Matrix*, taking the red pill and so on, that gave it away. Darus was always talking about that film.

Here was a dilemma. Ned didn't want to damage the reputation of Gear4u by failing to fulfil an order, but equally he didn't want to rip Darus off. After considering the matter for a few minutes, Ned sent this reply:

> Dear Gear4u customer,
> Thank you for your order. We have recently experienced problems with postal deliveries to the Stockwell area, with several parcels being seized at the sorting office. We are working to rectify this problem but for now we would recommend either providing another address for your order or ordering from another supplier. We apologise for any inconvenience this causes.
> Yours sincerely,
> Kira @ Gear4u

Darus replied ten minutes later:

> I'm real sorry to hear that. I don't have any other addresses to use so I will try another supplier. No worries. Thanks for your help. All best, DG.

It felt like a satisfying solution – an hour later, *BeastMode84* left a positive comment on Ned's supplier thread, praising his customer service – and yet for the rest of the day the incident left an uneasy feeling in Ned's mind. It made the people who were sending him money feel rather closer to home than he wanted them to be. It's not that he hadn't pictured their excitement at taking the risk of making the order, their anticipation and thrill at the arrival of the illicit parcel, their unpacking of the gear, their tremulous routines of injecting it. He had imagined all that, and had thought about their disappointment when they started to realise that the gear wasn't having any effect, that it might be bunk, but he didn't exactly want to think of them as real people whom he knew, who lived in flats just down the road from him, and who would have other pressing demands on their money. He didn't want to think about that.

GEAR4U WAS TRENDING: BY the end of the week, Ned's thread in Supplier Introductions sat at number one in the table of most viewed and replied-to threads that Roidsweb displayed at the side of the screen, and Gear4u was in the top five highest-rated suppliers on the site, with an average rating of 92.3%. The only thing that held Ned back from being number one was the fact that none of the real people who had bought gear from Gear4u had given it a product quality rating yet. On the fourth day of week one, Ned sent off seventeen orders and collected £1,825 in cash; on the fifth day, he sent off twenty-eight orders and collected £2,874; on the sixth day, he sent off thirty-three orders and collected £3,591. The women who worked behind the post office counter started to recognise him; they would cheerily go through the routine of asking whether he wanted to track the deliveries, and whether his parcels contained any valuables, knowing full well what he would say. 'More parcels? You ought to get yourself a franking machine, my love,' Margaret would say, or, 'Ooh, here's Mr Jiffy Bag again'. The young man with the turban who usually worked at the window for Western Union cash transfers treated him with increasing deference, perhaps impressed at, or suspicious about, the large amounts of cash he collected each day. Soon he had learned Ned's name: when the number came up and Ned came to his window, the man would be mouthing 'Brian Logan' to himself and typing it into his system before Ned had even got his ID out.

On the Sunday, when the post office was closed, Ned went back through his records and created a spreadsheet for the orders so far. The week's total was £16,560, with another £7,210 due to be collected by cash transfer on Monday. Ned had been keeping his bundles of notes in his underwear drawer, but he felt like he needed a better system now. He went back to Ryman's and bought another red metal money-box, like the one he used for his gear. When he got back to his bedsit, he took out the money while the light of the evening faded into dusk, and repacked it lovingly into the box, the greens, greys, purples and pinks neatly ordered and the coins snug in their layered compartments. The coins shone in the gloom.

NED WAS TRAINING WITH Darus again three days later; he had texted him the evening after receiving his order to set up the session. It was a chest-and-back day, starting with some heavy bench presses and wide-grip pull-ups. Darus was a little disappointed with how Ned's lifts had hit a plateau in the last weeks, since he dropped down to training two or three times a week, but Ned brushed it off: he was happy with his condition and the amount of time he put in at the gym.

Between sets they chatted. There was lots to talk about: in the month since they had seen each other, Ned had gone on leave, been made redundant, fallen out with Alice, reconciled with her, and gone live with Gear4u. He told Darus about the first four things.

'What are you going to do for work?' Darus asked.

'I'm going to bide my time for a while and think about it. I've got this redundancy payment coming which will last a few months, and I thought I might go live in a city where it'll last longer while I work things out.'

'Like a gap year?'

'Ha, I guess so. I never took a gap year. It might be a good time to take stock of things. Having turned thirty and all.'

'Man, I took a gap year sixteen years ago, thinking I would go back and graduate from high school, and I think I'm still on it. Just make sure you keep up your training. You got any idea where you'll go?'

'I was thinking of maybe going to Berlin,' Ned said. In the days since Alice had suggested it, he had been doing his research, and the idea had grown on him.

'I hear Berlin's cool. Never been myself, but I know people who have. I've seen photos where it's all, like, graffiti and street art everywhere. Is it cheap to live?'

'I think so. I know someone who's got this huge studio flat and she pays something like 500 euros a month for it. And buying a flat is much cheaper too.'

'You're thinking of buying? I can only dream of that, I don't know how I'd ever get a deposit together.'

'Well, unexpected things can happen if you want them to,' Ned said.

His final superset consisted of incline dumbbell flyes, supine rows, decline dumbbell presses and lower back reverse crunches with a 20-kilogram plate held to his chest. It was the conclusion of a well-designed work-out, challenging and varied, that brought Ned to exhaustion at the optimal point; his final reps in each set brought a low groan out of him, as he screwed up his face in concentration. 'See it through, Ned, come on!' Darus said. 'Hit that shit hard.'

Finally Ned finished the last reps. His chest felt destroyed, and when he drank his protein shake his body cried out for it, as if he could feel it going straight to his muscles. Darus sat with him in the changing room while he recovered. When the old man covered in tattoos had dried himself, dressed and left them alone, Ned asked Darus, 'Are you on cycle now?'

'Not yet. I had some source problems again. I've got enough to start off but I wanted to have it all in place for the whole four months before I begin. It's quite a big stack.'

'What was the source problem?'

'It's been various. Most recently I tried this new supplier everyone's raving about, but they said they couldn't fill out my order or they couldn't deliver it or something.'

To Ned, the feeling was delicious, possessing this secret knowledge and seeing it play out in Darus's life. He couldn't resist. 'I've got to let you in on something, man. That was me. I didn't want to mug you off, you see, that's why I didn't take your money.'

Darus seemed baffled. 'What's that?'

'It was me. On Roidsweb. BeastMode84?'

Now Darus looked irritated. ‘No, I’m BeastMode – it’s like SuperBeast Training, it’s part of my brand.’

‘No, yeah, I know that, but Gear4u – that’s me. Kira? I’m the one you were emailing.’

‘You asshole!’ – Darus broke into a smile.

‘I know, right?’

‘So what, you’ll give me the gear at cost price? Who’s your wholesaler?’

‘No, no, like I said, I don’t want to rip you off. The gear’s not real, it’s bunk. That’s why I didn’t sell it to you.’

‘Hang on. You’re telling me you’re selling gear that’s bunk and taking people’s money? Then how come everyone on the forum says the gear is so good?’

‘Some of that is real, because, I don’t know, people have convinced themselves that it’s good. But most of it is me, using different names.’

‘No fucking way.’

‘Yes way.’

‘No fucking *way*, man. That is genius.’

'IT'S LOOKING LIKE A bit of a triumph,' Alice said that evening. She and Ned were sitting in her flat; he had come over directly after the day's final trip to the post office, picking up a bottle of prosecco on the way to toast her successful audition and the launch of the website. 'I'm very impressed.'

'Cheers. And cheers to you on getting the part.' They clinked glasses; Ned sipped, swilled, held the liquid in his mouth and breathed in over it, tried to discern what he tasted, and gave up. 'Would you call this one biscuity or buttery?'

'More biscuity than buttery.' Alice sniffed her glass. 'Buttery is more Chardonnay. I suppose the tricky thing is that biscuits often taste buttery themselves.'

Ned smiled at her. Really she had been amazing in the last few weeks. Her acceptance of him. To Ned, now that he paused to think about it, it felt like a decisive change in his life, a decisive realisation: that if he told the things he felt most secretive or nervous or worried about to the person he most wanted to think well of him, those things would turn out not to be bad or shameful at all, but to be fine. In fact, he would find himself to be more likeable, perhaps even more loveable, because of having told them. Alice had an amazing capacity to surprise him. Last week when he'd told her how happy he was that she was so unworried about what he was doing with Gear4u, she shrugged, thought about it for a second or two and said, 'I suppose I'm pretty libertarian when it comes to that sort of thing really. Anyway, Bas and I always suspected that Daddy was a bit of a crook.'

'Go on,' Ned said.

'Well, one of his businesses was this so-called "building firm", but he'd clearly never been on a building site in his life. We'd get these brand-new JCBs randomly sitting in the old barn behind the wildflower meadow for a few weeks at a time, until some dodgy guy turned up with a big suitcase full of cash and took them away.'

'Really?'

'Well, maybe me and Bas imagined seeing the suitcases with our own eyes. But, yeah, I'm sure it was some sort of laundering thing. That's just capitalism though, isn't it? There's no difference really between being a landlord or a hedge fund manager or whatever, and selling JCBs to dodgy people for cash in hand.'

'I suppose not,' Ned said. 'It cracks me up how you say

"in the wildflower meadow", as if that's just a normal thing that people have in their gardens.'

Alice took the takeaway menu that she had been rolling up as she spoke, dug Ned in the ribs with it, and said, 'Shut up, you little oik.' Ned giggled. 'Living in a dungeony basement with a fucking sewage works running through it doesn't give you any street cred in my eyes.'

'Touché.'

Ned loved being teased by Alice. The first time she had visited the bedsit, she looked round and said, 'So, this is where the magic happens, is it?', and told Ned about how she had once lived in a basement room, after she drew the short straw in one of the houses she had shared with friends as a student – graciously not mentioning that while it was one thing for a twenty-year-old student to live in a short-straw basement in student housing before she got on with her adult, affluent life, it was quite another for a thirty-year-old to live here because it was all he could afford. She didn't seem to mind the place; she laughed the first time she heard the pipes gurgle. Still, spending time in Alice's lovely flat made Ned more determined to improve his lot.

And he had a nagging sense of something else he wanted to address. Since Alice got back in touch with him, they hadn't spoken about how things stood between them, though they now spent several evenings a week together. He wanted to avoid drifting into a situation without having decided whether he really wanted it or not. That had happened with Grace: they'd started sleeping together and before he knew it they were a couple, spending every weekend together, and dependent on each other in a way that he felt stifled by, and unable to change; clearly Grace had felt the same way too, since she broke up with him.

'You know when you talk about visiting me in Berlin, how do you see that going exactly?' Ned said.

'How do you mean?'

'Between us, I mean.'

'I hadn't really thought that far ahead. Goodness, this is very serious.' She pulled her legs up under her so she was sitting cross-legged, facing him on the sofa. 'How do *you* see things between us?'

'I just thought we should make sure we weren't giving each other any false impressions about what we wanted. For me, you know, I'm really into you and I'm having a terrific time, but I don't necessarily want to get into a monogamous relationship right now.'

'No, sure.'

'I mean, especially if I'm going to be moving somewhere else. So I really like how things are with us at the moment and I think we should keep things open in that way, you know?'

Ned had been looking towards the window as he spoke but now looked back to Alice, two feet away from him; she was smiling. 'You don't need to look so worried,' she said. 'Did you think I was going to become a ball and chain around your ankles?'

'Well, no, but—'

'It's fine, I'm totally happy keeping things open between us. That's better really, with the travelling I have to do for work. I'm glad we're having this conversation.'

'Me too.'

'You're very good at this kind of thing, you know.'

'What kind of thing?'

'At relationships. It's difficult to say to another person what it is that you really want, but you're good at just saying it like it is. It's quite hot, actually.'

'Come here,' Ned said.

Alice leaned in across the sofa towards him.

THE SITE REALLY EXPLODED towards the end of the second week. Ned dedicated himself to running Gear4u with total intensity and avidness: posting on the forums, replying to emails, collecting payments, parcelling up and sending off orders. Each day he went to the post office three times, and each time he carried more and more jiffy bags in his rucksack.

THE PHONE RANG. NED had left it on his bedside table on the other side of the room while he sat at the desk; he finished writing, clicked 'Publish' on a forum post, and picked it up on the seventh ring. Darus.

'Can we meet?'

'Umm . . . I'm a little busy at the moment, Darus.'

'It's just, I gotta talk to you about something.'

'Okay, well, I could talk after our next session – did we put that in the diary yet? Maybe in a fortnight or so?'

'You know, I really want to talk before that.'

'We're talking now, right? So what is it?'

'I was really hoping to do this in person, Ned.'

Outside, the brakes of a bus hissed and scraped. Ned sensed an edge in Darus's voice that he hadn't heard there before. 'As I say, Darus, I'm pretty busy at the moment.'

'If you want to do this now, okay then. I gotta tell you, I've been looking at the Gear4u website and it's quite an operation you've got going there. Quite an operation. You've done really well. I mean, it makes me wish I'd had the chance to get to know so much about computers and programming and all that shit.'

'Umm, thanks, Darus. It's going well.'

'And you deserve a lot of credit for that. A lot of credit. All the technical know-how to make that website and email accounts and whatnot, all those names you came up with for the feedback.'

'Yeah, thanks a lot, Darus. It's good of you to say that.'

'How do you think up all that stuff? You must have dozens of profiles on there, right, to have so much kudos?'

'It's just being creative with it, really. It's like any creative endeavour, you have to go into it with imaginative depth –'

'Right, right,' Darus was saying, though Ned got the sense that he wasn't fully listening.

'– and some people are just naturally inventive, I guess.'

'Right, right,' Darus said. 'You know, what I was thinking was, we really ought to talk about the arrangement going forward.'

'How do you mean?'

'You see, you say that it's all because you're just so imaginative, but I distinctly remember a conversation where I told you exactly how it could be done. I told you it would be easy to sell fake gear on there. Right? You remember?'

'Well, it wasn't exactly like that—'

'I sure remember. We were standing right there by the squat rack, I remember it well. And then I remember a little while later I also told you how to get a fake ID, and I thought at the time, "Hey, I wonder what he's up to".'

'Look, Darus, that's not quite how it went, is it? I mean, the idea itself is nothing; it could occur to anyone.'

'The idea is everything, Ned.'

'No, it's . . .' Ned hesitated, annoyed to find his voice coming out squeakily, and Darus cut him off.

'The idea is everything, and it was my idea, and I could have got any one of a dozen people to do for me what you've done. Do you know how many programmer nerds are out there? You're basically like my technician on this. That's all you are.'

Ned felt a tight constriction in his throat. He wanted to scream but he knew that he must not allow himself. Composure, composure. Deliberately he took a long breath down into his belly and clenched his stomach muscles when he replied: 'Darus, I don't think there's anything to discuss here, and I'm actually in the middle of something, so I really need to go.'

'Oh, really? Because I think there's a lot more to discuss. A hell of a lot. And I'll tell you this for free, I'm not letting this go until I get my fucking cut for what was my idea.'

Pause.

'How much do you think your cut should be?'

'I want sixty per cent of everything you've made from it.'

'Darus, that's completely—'

'Sixty per cent, Ned. Or I go to the police with what I know.'

Ned hung up.

WHILE HE CARRIED ON running Gear4u in the third week since the site went live, Ned took stock of the situation in his mind. He looked at how much he had achieved in the last months, creating the whole enterprise out of nothing. It had been a wonderful time. Never before had he had such free rein to exercise his creativity and intelligence, to see through a project of his own from first conception to successful completion, with full creative control. He couldn't let Darus ruin it for him now. He had to keep hold of the situation. It was stupid of him to have told Darus about it at all. An unnecessary risk. Showing off!

Ned told Alice about Darus's call. 'Oh, what an absolute cunt,' she said, and told Ned that he should just ignore Darus or string him along until he'd worked out a way to fend him off. The more Ned told himself that he could find a way to neutralise Darus's threat, and the more he visualised how he might do it, the more he felt that the odds were on his side. But Alice was right, he needed to keep Darus quiet for now. He needed to let him think he was winning, so that he wouldn't do anything drastic – go to the police, or blow Ned's cover on Roidsweb – while Ned worked out what to do. On Tuesday of week three, he sent Darus a text saying that on consideration, the proposal seemed fair, and that he would sort it out by the end of the week.

An hour later, he had a new feedback report on Roidsweb from *BeastMode84*. It was the most enthusiastic review he'd ever received, stronger in its praise than he had ever dared to be in the reviews he wrote himself. Things were looking good then; Darus was onside.

As NED HAD EXPECTED, by the middle of the third week, a few forum members had started to express doubts about the quality of his products. *GhostDog*, one of his earliest customers, wrote,

> Been pinning Gear4u's Deca and Test for eight days now @ 500 mg each split into two pins p.w. but not feeling anything at all. No pump, no boost in my lifts, no nothing. I'm not even getting morning wood like I normally do on cycle. Anyone else thinking this shit might be under-dosed or is it just me?

Ned immediately used four of his sockpuppets to down-vote this post, then logged in as *joey deacon* and wrote:

> fuckin amature's like this do my head in. earth to gay dog: if you;ve been pinning it for eight days, ITS TOO EARLY TO KNOW WHAT THE EFFECT IS YET. everyone nows gear takes 12 to 14 days to stablelize increased hormone levels. do your research before criticising a

supplier with ignorant shit like this!! or you don't belong on here at all!

GhostDog fairly quickly replied, 'Woah man, no need to chew me out, I'm just saying my experiences here.' In reply to this, Ned got *Trans Guy* to say to *GhostDog*, 'joey might be harsh but he's telling it straight up in this case: you haven't been pinning long enough to say for sure this is bunk, and you shouldn't go around accusing a start-up source of being sub-standard until you've been using their gear for three weeks', and then, as *Mr_MXYZPTLK*, he wrote, 'Just wanted to add that I've been using the same products as Ghost for twelve days and the results are great so far, big pumps and I'm getting that real swollen, full-of-life feeling coming on strong!'

As Kira, Ned replied to *Ghost Dog* to say that Gear4u worked hard to ensure the quality of all their products, and would happily send free replacements for any vials which people could prove to be under-dosed by producing a valid lab report on the levels of active hormone in the oil. It was a double bluff: he knew that nobody would go to the trouble of paying a lab or a compounding pharmacy to run tests on a controlled substance that had been sold to them illegally.

Having quelled this early doubt, in the next days Ned

drowned out the unhappy customers with contradictory positive reports. He had 20 more accounts now for a total of 170. Five of them were run by Alice. She'd said she wanted to help with the project, and Ned was doubtful at first, but she proved to be really good at generating convincing material for her sockpuppets. Her major persona was a female bodybuilder called *Alice*. She was sharp-witted and didn't take any shit from the men on the forums. Alice found that the direct messages inbox for *Alice* was soon groaning with flirtatious or obscene messages; she didn't reply to them, which sometimes provoked further aggressive follow-up messages, but she read some of them aloud to Ned in absurd voices. Alice and Ned's sockpuppets would conduct long, involved discussions among themselves about the qualities of the different product lines they had ordered from Gear4u: which was giving them more bloated or leaner gains; which was giving more or less PIP (post-injection pain); which was giving them bigger pumps, and making them more horny. But the tide was starting to turn; the negative reviews were driving his kudos down. By the end of the third week, Gear4u had slipped from first position among UK sources to fourth.

That Saturday, Ned received an email from a customer telling him that instead of his delivery he'd had a parcel seizure notice come through his door. He was going spare with worry: that the police would come to his house and make enquiries; that they'd search his internet records, tell his employer; that they'd come when his wife was at home, she'd answer the door and everything would be ruined . . . Ned immediately sent a refund of his cash transfer, and wrote a reassuring message, telling him that his order was practically untraceable, the police would have no way of proving that the package hadn't been sent to him without his knowledge, and, anyway, possession of class-C controlled substances was basically decriminalised.

The seizure notice gave Ned pause. Surely his packaging was totally discreet; why would a post office have suspicions? But he couldn't start worrying about that now. That evening, Ned did his accounts for the week and found that the volume of orders was still growing, even if the increase of the growth rate was slowing down.

One morning in mid-July, the fourth week after the site had gone live, as Ned was busy fighting the gradual decline of Gear4u's reputation and Alice was keeping an eye on the inbox for him, she looked across from the sofa and said, 'Hmmm. I think you ought to read this one.'

'Oh yes?'

She handed him the laptop, with a direct message from Best British Steroids opened in full screen. This was the supplier from which Ned had made his original order, back when the whole business was thrilling, terrifying and new to him. Best British Steroids had been the most highly rated UK-based supplier on Roidsweb when Ned started Gear4u.

Hi Kira and all at gear4u.

It looks like you're running a great operation there – congratulations on that. The way you're doing customer service and brand management is an inspiration to us all – Even if you do seem to have taken some of my business! But I can't help noticing you seem to be having some batch quality problems, with these disfavourable reviews creeping in. Are you satisfied with your producer? I wouldn't want the quality of a great operation to be hit by gear that turns out to be bunk.

I run a complete operation here, producing and selling, but I'm looking to expand. I know I'm better at the production than the marketing and I'm overstretched to do both. Let me know if you'd be interested in collaborating. Or even teaming up! It would be an honour to work with such a professional outfit as gear4u.

Yours sincerely,

Jason at BBS

Ned stood and paced back and forth, biting his knuckle in concentration. 'You look like you're doing a charade of someone deep in thought,' Alice said.

'Ha,' Ned said flatly. 'I'm trying to work out what this means. Whether it's trustworthy. It seems weird to me.'

'What's weird about it? Sit down anyway, you're making me nervous.'

Ned sat. 'What's weird is the timing – just after we had a parcel seized, and just as some people are starting to twig that the gear might be bunk.'

'Yeah, but that's why he's written to you. And the parcel thing could just be a coincidence.'

'It could. But Best British Steroids has gone totally quiet

on the forums recently. They were the top supplier six months ago and they've almost vanished. Then they turn up out of the blue with this. It makes me suspicious. It makes me wonder if the person behind it has been busted, and the cops are trying to roll him over to help catch other suppliers.'

'Gosh,' Alice said.

Ned sent Best British Steroids a reply saying, 'Thank you. But how do I know you're not law enforcement?'

Across several messages in the next few hours, Jason tried to convince Ned that this wasn't a set-up, that they could safely meet in person and be business partners. Well, maybe it was a set-up, maybe it wasn't, but it was enough to spook Ned. He imagined turning up for a rendezvous with 'Jason' and having a team of drug squad officers arrest him. Was that how it would happen? The quiet tap on the shoulder from the plain-clothes officer, the sudden discreet flash of his policeman's badge. *Can you come this way, sir?* The more Ned thought about it, the more his mind got to work on scenarios. They would search his bedsit and find the cash and the supplies; they would seize his computer and get into the Gear4u control panel; they would match up the domain registered under the fake ID with the Western Union collections under the same name, and they would arrest him. He found himself sweating heavily into his t-shirt just thinking about it.

A TEXT FROM DARUS: 'HEY Ned, can we meet to go over accounts this evening and work out how much you owe me? Is the money still in cash?'

Ned knew he needed to act now. After a week and a half, Darus's texts were becoming more frequent; he couldn't dead-bat them for much longer. He tried to work out how much Darus knew about him. He certainly knew his email address and mobile number, and Ned had mentioned the part of town he lived in – it was only fifteen minutes' walk from the gym – but Ned didn't think he'd ever given Darus his address. It would be on file at SunFit though. All Darus needed to do was sweet-talk one of the receptionists into calling up Ned's membership details on the computer for him. And did Darus know where he worked? Probably not, but there weren't that many design agencies in the neighbourhood either; it wouldn't be difficult to track him down through his colleagues. His ex-colleagues, he would soon have to say – Ned was counting the days until his final pay packet and redundancy money arrived in his account.

If he could find a way to neutralise Darus's threat to go

to the police, while also keeping him from exposing him on Roidsweb for long enough that Ned could see the project through . . . if he could get Darus off his back for good, while also keeping all the money for himself . . . what he needed was some way to ensure that Darus wouldn't, or couldn't, go to the police. The outline of a plan was forming in his mind.

Ned walked to the post office to collect his latest takings. A hip-looking middle-aged couple were struggling to control their whippet as it lunged for fried chicken bones on the pavement, almost tripping Ned up and causing a group of teenage girls to scatter, giggling. No, the whole thing was getting too risky, it was crazy; all it would take was for one aggrieved customer to tip off the police, or Western Union, or the post office, that this branch was being used for cash pick-ups for drugs . . . or for one aggrieved customer to stake out the post office themselves . . . And then there were the strange messages about the seizure and the buy-out. Were the police trying to trap him already? In any case, the thought of having Darus breathing down his neck found Ned clenching his jaw into a rictus of anxiety. He had to act. He texted Darus back to say sure, he would come round at seven o'clock that evening.

Five hours later he was walking to Darus's place in Stockwell. He popped into the off-licence to get some beers and Kettle chips but as he stood in the queue his eyes drifted to the wine fridge and he thought, fuck it, let's buy a bottle of champagne. He realised this was something he had never done before. That couldn't be right, could it, to get to thirty without ever having bought a bottle of champagne? But he was an adult, he had credit cards. He put the beers back in place, walked to the fridge and, with a gleeful sense of freedom, decided to buy the most expensive thing on offer, whatever it was. A magnum of pink Laurent-Perrier: fine. The fridge door didn't budge so he yanked at it in frustration, making the whole unit rock on its heels and the woman behind the counter shout, '*It's padlocked!* I'll come when I've served these customers.' Ned waited for her, feeling somewhat embarrassed, but observing his own embarrassment with amusement. The bottle looked enormous when it was sitting on the counter in front of him, and even bigger when the woman had tucked it into its big, square-cornered gift box.

Ned buzzed at Darus's intercom and the lock clicked open instantly. The champagne didn't seem to make any impression on Darus; he already had a tin of lager on the go, and offered one to Ned, who took it and put the magnum in Darus's fridge. They could have that later. First they would get down to business.

'So you've come round to my way of thinking about the split?'

'Yeah. I mean, I was against it at first, but when I thought about it, I thought fair enough, I guess it was his idea. And it's true I didn't know anything about that whole world before you introduced me to it.'

'And you're good with sixty per cent?'

'Sure.'

'Good man. Cheers to that.'

They tapped their tins against each other and shook hands. Darus sat back, puffed his cheeks out, and said with a smile and a slight shake of the head, 'Okay, now we've shaken on it, I've got to tell you, you're a fucking awful negotiator, Ned.'

'You think?'

'Yeah, man. You just gave into me straight away without a counter-offer. If we're going to be in this together going forward, you've got to be a lot tougher with people.'

Ned was crushing his empty tin in his hand, allowing the familiar feeling of being patronised by Darus to play across his thoughts and come to rest. What a real prick Darus could be. What an absolute grade-A knob. 'I'll crack open that champagne, yeah,' Ned said, 'and we can toast the website?'

Ned could feel the beer, drunk quickly on an empty stomach, taking its effect on him already, as if his balance were entering the kitchen a split second after the rest of his body. He took the magnum from the fridge, set it down on the counter and was studying the flaps on the top of the box when Darus called through from the front room, 'How're things with Alice?'

'Oh, they're good, thanks. She's amazing.'

'She certainly must have been a real hottie in her youth.'

'What do you mean? She's only twenty-nine, and she's still getting modelling work.'

'I dunno, man, I always thought her eyes were a bit funny. They have that sort of hooded thing, right? And when a woman starts getting towards thirty, things can get pretty saggy. Slack. You know what I mean?'

'That's ridiculous,' Ned said. He had taken the foil off the bottle and was carrying it in to the front room on a tray with two glasses; Darus was sitting at his laptop, facing away from him.

'No way, man,' he said. 'When the thirties come round it all gets pretty fucking slack down there. All it takes is for her to have been filled in by a couple of black guys, and you won't even be touching the sides.'

Darus laughed obscenely, with his back still turned away. Ned felt his hatred for him spit white-hot like a flame. How dare he? Who the fuck did he think he was? Ned had set the tray down and picked the magnum up, when the image arose in his mind of how easily he could take the neck of the bottle in two hands, hoist it upside down, draw it back round his side like a baseball bat, shift his momentum through his hips and feet, and swing the bottle forward with all his weight behind it. He pictured the blow thudding against the side of Darus's head; Darus being knocked from his chair, lying flat on his back on the Ikea rug; Ned leaning over him to see the right side of his face caved in, his eye socket, cheek bone and brow a pink mess, all collapsed in on themselves, as if the stuffing had been knocked out of him; an area of blood spreading from his matted hair into the rug . . .

'Don't worry, man, I'm just fucking with you,' Darus said, breaking the silence, and he swung round in his chair. 'She's gorgeous really. Are you going to do the honours?'

Ned twisted the cork out methodically, taking a deep breath and feeling his pulse rate coming back down to normal. He poured out two tumblers of champagne, having failed to find any flutes or wine glasses in Darus's cupboard, and offered one to Darus. As they clinked glasses, Ned savoured the knowledge that in a few minutes' time he would never see Darus again.

Back home an hour later, Ned opened up the Gear4u administrator page. He still had the details of every Western

Union transfer that had been made to him in the last month. He opened the first one – Dave Galvin – took a screencap of the transfer details, opened it as a JPEG and clicked 'Edit'. If he changed the name 'Brian Logan', the name under which the money had been collected, to 'Darus Gaynesford', there was a good chance that Darus would believe it. The text looked like it was in Arial; Ned placed a white rectangle over the old name and typed 'Darus Gaynesford' in ten-point Arial where it had been. It looked perfect, totally authentic. He saved the edited image, attached it to a new message in Hushmail, and drafted an email to Darus:

Darus,

Forget sixty per cent, you can have my final offer on the split now: nothing. I won't be giving you any money, and see the attached image for the reason why you can't go to the police or expose me on Roidsweb. The whole operation has been run in your name from the beginning. Since the end of May, more than 200 cash transfers have been sent to, and collected by, 'Darus Gaynesford', using an ID card in that name. If you continue to contact me, I will anonymously pass this information on to the police, SunFit, all major gym chains and the personal training community. Let's see what they all make of that.

Best wishes,

N

ON THE SUNDAY AFTERNOON of the fourth week since going live, Ned gave himself a few hours off from Roidsweb and Gear4u.

A sunny, late-July afternoon. That morning he had slept in late. Alice was away filming her pilot. Ned hadn't done much except start a thread headed 'I pinned my dog', under the user name *Flash*:

> He's my buddy, he's my faithful companion, I had him before either of my boys and I do love this dog immensely, some may feel its reckless, some may not understand, some may think its a waste of good juice, but three weeks ago I gave the ole boy 50 mg of deca and 50 mg of test, he's creeping up on 14 and I see the change in him, I have to carry him up the stairs sometimes and lift him in and out of the truck, he still seems happy to be around but it tears me apart to see him sluggish, maybe its wishful thinking, but I swear he seems more perky already, he is much more livelier, he's been doing a lot of funny stuff, his hormones make him think he's a young pup again and

> can bang all the bitches so to speak and also the table legs lol, I'm planning on this low dose once a week for a few months

Ned refrained from replying to it; he wanted to see how the real forum members would react. Within five minutes, it had its first two replies: *Mr Anonymous* wrote, 'Oh you fucking crazy fuck you! Have you got him on a weights routine yet?'; while *Overhard* wrote: 'Lol, you are really a research scientist. People tests on rats, and you've moved onto dogs.'

Leaving his phone at home, Ned went out for a walk. He looked at the furniture in the window of the fancy design store that had opened on the high street and popped in to the newsagent for a copy of the *Observer* and a packet of chewing gum. Carrying on to the coffee shop, he bought a Danish pastry and a coffee, and walked until he found himself down by the entrance to the park. He found a bench and sat down to read the paper while eating the Danish and drinking the coffee. He started with the property section, the part of the paper he had always ignored until recently, but now studied closely. Then sports. The Olympics were starting next week, and the paper was full of news; Ned had been so absorbed in other things, it took him by surprise that it was so close.

At home, Ned found a text from Alice containing a photo of the catering table at the set and the caption, 'Fuck me, the spread is amazing', and also a text from Grace. Grace wondered how he was, and if he wanted to go for lunch with her one day next week. Interesting. He texted her back suggesting Wednesday.

He then went back to Roidsweb. 'I pinned my dog' was doing well: the initial post had a 95 per cent kudos rating, and it was the most viewed thread in the General Discussion area. *Testo Junkie* expressed the feelings of the majority when he wrote, 'I was a bit taken back when I first read the title to this thread, but now that I've gone through it, I can't believe I never thought of it myself before. Homebrew TRT for dogs! Kudos, brother!'

Ned decided to step into the debate. As *Jack Daniels*, he wrote:

> Damn, I'm sorry man. I know it can be REALLY hard when a dog that you've had for so long starts to show signs of old age. What you're doing sounds like a great idea for him, Deca will definitely help with his joints and maneuverability. What kind of dog is he, may I ask, and how big? And where are you pinning him? I wonder if 50/50 of deca/test might be a little much. It might be worth it to dial

> it down and see if it gives him the energy you want without the alpha dog side effects.

Ned quickly replied to this as *Kaden* with, 'The forum hereby names him AlphaDog', went back to the window where he was logged in as *Flash*, and wrote:

> He's a border collie, so he used to jump really high and run very fast, he is almost 80 lbs, I use a slin pin and shoot him in the meatyest part of his hind quarter, I guess like the top of his thigh, he's a smart dog, he sees me getting the slin pins out and he hangs right next to me, even when I'm doing my injections he comes to look, and I have to tell him his is later lololol

When Ned updated his spreadsheet that evening, he discovered with delight that the revenue from the 492 legitimate orders he had received so far totalled £67,470, most of which he had already collected in cash. In the moneybox he kept under his bed, the rows of banknotes were several inches thick. He liked to take them out, squeeze their fatness, feel the give in the stacks of glossy cotton, and slap them against his palm with a dense sound.

Ned's phone buzzed just as he was getting into bed, and he found a text message from Darus: 'You win this time, asshole, but if I ever see you at the club again I'm gonna kick ur ass so fucken hard'.

So Ned had won. He repeated softly to himself, *I won, I won*, and tried to enjoy the moment as he drifted off to sleep.

WOKEN BY THE BUZZ of the intercom, Ned groped his way across the room, picked up the receiver, became blearily aware that he was naked and had a very hard erection, and said, 'Hello?'

'Hello, this is Special Police Constable Deborah Kersey. Could I speak to the occupier, please?'

Ned froze. 'Just give me a minute,' he managed to say in a hollow voice, and placed the receiver down. Oh god, he'd been so stupid. How could he possibly have thought he would get away with it? He felt sick. He felt ridiculous, standing there with a twanging hard-on, now slowly starting to subside. He climbed into the jeans and pulled on the sweatshirt that he had draped over the back of his chair last night. What to do? There was no exit from the building other than the front door. Ned looked despairingly at the bars across his basement window. Maybe he could just sit tight, and she would go away. How long could he brazen it out for? But if they really wanted him they would smash the front door in. Oh god, they're probably waiting to do that now. Jesus Christ. Ned sat down on the sofa. If he could only think, think, think, he would find a solution. But the intercom buzzed again, shattering his concentration. There was nothing for it. She wasn't going away.

Ned opened the door and started up the stairs. The security lights on the stairwell didn't come on; Ned windmilled his arms to trigger the sensor; the lights clicked on, and he was caught in the harsh glare. At the front door he halted. He slid the cap that covered the peephole aside and saw the policewoman's image bulging towards him, grotesquely enlarged and distorted by the convex lens. Here it was. He'd sometimes wondered if this moment would come. But now it was real. Ned opened the door and stared at her, paralysed.

'Hello. I'm very sorry to bother you so early on a Monday morning, sir. I'm SPC Kersey and I work with the Safer Neighbourhood Team in this ward. I'm investigating reports from some of your neighbours of anti-social and threatening behaviour from youths in this area, especially on Patmore Road. Have you witnessed anything of that kind recently?'

Ned couldn't help giving out a gleeful laugh. Reprieved, he thought. He was free! He smiled easily, feeling fully in control of the situation, tilted his head to one side, and said, 'Oh, no, I wouldn't say that at all. There are kids who hang round in the street in the evenings, and outside the chicken shop round the corner, but they certainly don't bother me.

They're just smoking and talking and riding their bikes. They're fine.'

'Okay, thanks. That's what most people have been saying too, but as I say, we've had these reports, and I do have to investigate them.'

'Yes, I see. But I really think people are worrying about nothing.'

The woman gave Ned a sympathetic look, which Ned took as tacit acknowledgement that she was on his side, she wasn't one of the stuck-up people who were afraid of black teenagers either. Ned smiled back, and it occurred to him that she was really quite sexy when you looked beyond her ugly, ill-fitting uniform. He wondered if he should make a pass at her.

'Is there anything else you'd like to discuss with me today?' she said.

'No, no. Everything's fine.'

'Okay then. Have a good day.'

Then she was gone, and Ned was on his own, feeling absurd, giddy and wired at what had just happened. He got back in bed, tried and failed to get back to sleep, and decided to call Alice on Facetime. Fifteen seconds later she appeared on his screen looking gorgeously dishevelled, her bare shoulders emerging from crisp white bedsheets.

IT WAS THAT NIGHT, lying awake in bed, that Ned realised he was ready to walk away from the whole thing. Fuck Jason from Best British Steroids, he thought. Fuck Darus. Fuck Roidsweb, fuck Gear4u. Fuck the police. He was tired of it all. He had been running the operation non-stop for ten weeks now, with barely a day off from the forums. But he could walk away. The realisation sent a wave of excitement through his body.

He got out of bed, dressed and sat at his desk. 1:30 a.m., his phone said, but he felt clear-headed and awake. He deleted the Gear4u website and his Gear4u account on Roidsweb; within an hour, all three had disappeared. He moved everything he wanted to keep from his MacBook onto a flashdrive, shut down, and found the tiny screwdriver he needed to open up his machine; within five minutes he had the back of the casing off and the hard drive removed. He triple-bagged the laptop and the hard drive in Sainsbury's bags knotted at the top, propped them at an angle between wall and floor and – fuck it, he needed a new laptop anyway – he gave them both a kicking, jumping on them, dropkicking and toe-punting them, until the hard drive seemed to have snapped, and the computer had at least bent a bit, and made some satisfyingly crunchy noises. Then he left the house with the two bags, dropped the smaller one containing the hard drive in the bin two streets away and dropped the larger one in the bin on the main road.

Back home, Ned took all the supplies that remained from Gear4u out of the bottom of his wardrobe – the remaining bottle of grapeseed oil, the vials, needles, syringes, packaging, compliment slips and fake ID – and dumped them on his bed. The pile looked surprisingly small; he had sent out almost everything he had in stock. With a Stanley knife he scratched the photograph of his face from the ID card and cut the neck of the bottle open, then pushed all the rest of the supplies inside it, before putting the whole thing inside his holdall from the gym, and wrapping the holdall inside two black bin liners. Shortly after midnight he set out up the high street, walked for ten minutes and turned right into Hancock Road, where it didn't take him very long to find one among the long line of big detached houses which had a half-full builder's skip out the front. He buried the whole lot under some rubble in the skip. It would soon be in a landfill.

Ned could imagine how pissed off the people who had sent the final cash transfers and never received any gear were going to be. They would trash Gear4u's reputation, threaten violence. But when he thought it out rationally, he knew that the closest anyone could get to finding him was the fact that the deliveries had been stamped and sent out by his local sorting office. Anyone who had received an order from him would be able to narrow it down to his postcode, but no further. It was possible, if the police were interested, that they could have been watching the post office, that they could interview the people who worked behind the counters, or watch the CCTV tapes to try to identify the person collecting the cash transfers for the name on the fake ID. But none of that seemed likely.

Other forum posters would speculate that Ned had been busted, he knew. They would wonder whether this signalled a tougher approach to policing steroid suppliers. But when Gear4u had been silent for a month or two, Ned knew people would forget about it. It was normal for suppliers to shut down suddenly; others always came in to fill the gap. Other scammers would probably try to do what Ned had done. From time to time, someone on the forums would wonder why a particular forum member – *joey deacon*, or *Kaden*, or *Roider of the Lost Ark* – had gone so quiet, but Ned doubted that anybody would notice the larger pattern, that 190 forum members who had joined between March and early July 2012 had all suddenly gone silent on the same day, never logging in again. The forums were busy enough that this could pass unnoticed. Ned imagined visiting Roidsweb sometimes, without logging in, to look back at old threads on the forums, and finding all his characters still there, poised mid-banter or argument or training update, like the crew on a ghost ship.

GRACE WAS ALREADY AT the restaurant when Ned arrived for their lunch, sitting in a shiny, brass-railed booth at the back of the room with her head leant over a book. They greeted each other, Ned settled in next to her, Grace ordered a bottle of Picpoul, and when the waiter had walked away, Ned mimicked his way of saying, 'An excellent choice, madam.'

Grace giggled, gestured at him to shush, carefully filled up their water glasses, and said to Ned, 'So how's life?' It was clear from her bright-eyed manner that she was fishing for gossip.

Ned gave a vague answer, and Grace said with a smile, 'Are you seeing anyone?'

'I wondered if you knew,' Ned said.

'Well, I only heard about you and Alice recently,' Grace said. 'But how come you met her? We've hardly been in touch in the last few years.'

'We go to the same gym, or we did until recently. One day she said hello. To be honest, I didn't recognise her, or realise that we'd met before, until she told me who she was.'

'And is it going well?'

'Yeah. It is. She's really terrific. Well, you know that already. But it's not necessarily that serious a thing. We're keeping options open at the moment, that's what both of us want.'

Grace was smiling to herself. While she gently twirled the stem of her wine glass, watching the liquid wash up the sides of the glass and run down in legs, Ned studied her heart-shaped face. How pretty she was! It felt to Ned like he had forgotten this about her, or allowed it to become distorted by all the other thoughts and feelings he associated with her. Yet here she was: those angular cheekbones, that soft bloom on her skin, the flecks of gold or honey in her amber eyes. She looked up at him, still smiling, and he was reminded of how she would sometimes look at him when she was sucking his cock.

'What is it?' said Ned.

'Nothing. It's just – I'm surprised, that's all. You know, I always liked Alice a lot, but it seemed like she was sort of in a different world from the rest of us. Even when we were at college, she would be disappearing off in the middle of term for skiing weekends with her boyfriends, and they were always, like, hedge-fund managers or something. When she came to our parties there was a sense that she was being a good sport, like a sort of visiting dignitary being very nice and tolerant of all the normal people before going back to her real life. It just seems strange that she's seeing my ex-boyfriend. Or, you know, "keeping her options open" with him.'

Ned couldn't recall now why he had been worried about Grace finding out that he was seeing Alice. No, of course she wasn't jealous or upset, or at least, those weren't her main feelings; he had misunderstood this about relationships between women. Rather, the idea that he was seeing Alice, after Grace had dumped him, flattered Grace's sense of herself, and elevated him in her estimation. Ned raised an eyebrow and said, 'You mean, you're surprised I could pull someone so far out of my league?'

'I didn't say *that* exactly. But, yes, it is a bit surprising. Maybe I underestimated you. Anyway, it seems like you've changed a lot. You seem a lot happier. It's really nice to see.'

'Thank you,' Ned said, feeling unexpectedly moved. 'I am a lot happier. And you know, some of those things you said to me when we broke up . . . I know I didn't say anything at the time but I saw how true they were, and I've tried to take that on board, I suppose.'

'Well, I'm really glad to see you doing so well. And I have to say, you're looking very hunky these days.'

'Thank you. You're looking in great shape yourself. Are you still doing yoga?'

Grace told him about the development of her yoga training, spin classes and climbing weekends in the last few months, before they spoke about recent news from some of her friends, and her work at the charity, which she was about to give up. Then Grace asked Ned about his work – how come he was free for lunch in the middle of the day? He told her that he had taken voluntary redundancy, and was contemplating having a career break.

'But what will you do?' Grace said.

He said that he was thinking of moving to Berlin.

'But I mean, what will you do for money?'

He said he was sure he'd get by.

'I can't believe it. It's not like you to be so relaxed about it. You were always so stressed about being in your overdraft.'

'I know I was,' Ned said. 'I'm sorry that I must have been such a drag. I feel a lot better about that stuff now. And there'll always be work for freelance web developers in Berlin if I want to go back to that. I've looked into it.'

Grace told Ned that she had some news too. She had been offered representation by a gallery in Edinburgh, and was going to have three of her paintings in a group show there, curated by one of her heroes, next year. Ned stood up to embrace her, feeling a surge of delight and affection. Throughout the time when they were dating, Grace had been fretting about her future, how she wasn't getting any interest from galleries and wasn't managing to sell any work herself; this arrangement sounded perfect for her, a total triumph. Grace seemed taken aback at the warmth of Ned's congratulations. Also, she said, her other news was that she had split up with Federico, whom she had started to find a bit boring, a bit lacking in dynamism.

An hour later, she and Ned were back in his bedsit, lying on their sides on the bed and kissing. He had his shirt off, and Grace was wearing nothing but her bra and knickers.

'I've got my period at the moment,' she said.

'I don't mind that.'

'Well, I do. It's too heavy, it would be gross. But we can do other things.'

She swivelled her hip towards Ned, moved his hand from where it lay on her waist towards her backside, and wriggled back against it. With his index finger he stroked the thin cotton of her knickers, traced the way the curves of her backside met, and found the firm nub of muscle in the centre. Gently he pressed against it; she gave out a shiver of excitement and whispered to him, 'You can do that, you know. Do you have any lube?'

GRACE HAD LEFT, AND Ned was sitting at his desk. He hadn't turned the lights on, although the sun was now starting to dim, or tidied up the bedsheets that were still coiled in a sweaty mess where they'd been trodden down at the foot of the bed, or washed or dressed himself beyond putting on a pair of jeans. He wanted to stretch this moment out for longer, to use it as a vantage point.

He could see the future all laid out before him. If he added his cash from Gear4u to his redundancy payment, it came to more than £85,000. A few minutes' research online told him that if he could somehow get the cash into a bank account without arousing suspicion or paying taxes, it would convert into enough Euros – more than 100,000, if he didn't lose too much on the exchange – to buy outright a small, one-bedroom apartment in an up-and-coming part of Berlin. He wouldn't even need a mortgage. He would go to Berlin, find work as a developer there to earn enough money to cover his living costs, and live cheaply.

In a few months' time, then, he could be a property owner. He pictured an apartment, large and high-ceilinged, with white walls, sturdy pine floorboards, and a few items of well-chosen vintage furniture. He inserted himself into the scene, pictured himself leaning back on a green leather sofa, flicking through a German dictionary, dressed in a pair of light, oatmeal-coloured linen trousers and a well-cut t-shirt. His front room would face into a quiet courtyard in an early twentieth-century building, with food markets, cinemas and coffee shops on his doorstep; there would be a view of the television tower from his bedroom window. In fact, now that he thought about it, if he could save up some more money for a deposit, after a while he could probably rent out his first apartment to somebody and use the rental income to buy a second place. Prices in Berlin were bound to go up, it was obvious. Or he could keep both apartments and rent them out one at a time for short-term holiday lets. British and American people would pay a ridiculous amount of money for that.

But he shouldn't get greedy. He should remain appreciative, grateful, proud of how much he had achieved. He should allow himself to enjoy the things he had earned. His life in Berlin could be exactly as he wanted it to be, with pleasure and purposefulness perfectly balanced: he would wake early, eat a simple breakfast, go to the gym in the morning, do some freelance work, read a novel or improve his German in the middle of the day, visit galleries in the late afternoon, cook meals in the evening, see friends and go on dates by night, just as he had a mind to.

Alice had said she would come and visit him as often as she could. He thought about Alice, whom he hadn't seen in more than a week now, and his cock started to thicken again, even though he was still feeling a little tender from Grace and smelling amazingly of her. If Alice moved to LA, as she'd occasionally suggested that she would, then Ned could pay return visits to her there. How cool would that be? He had never been to America. He imagined casually telling one of the bored expats at a dinner party in Berlin, *Oh, didn't I mention? – I'm off to LA next week, yeah I'll be staying with an actress friend out there . . .*

But in Berlin, anyway, between Alice's visits he would date other women too. He would tell them at the outset that he wasn't interested in a monogamous relationship, and he'd only go further with things if they were okay with that. He didn't want to be callous with anybody's feelings. But he definitely felt like he hadn't fucked enough women yet. Maybe in ten years' time he would want to settle down and have children, but for now why would he want to limit himself, why would he want to narrow down possibilities, when the whole shining world was within his reach?

That reminded him, he must check the details of his notice period on the bedsit. He thought it was just one month now, on a periodic tenancy. And he should look at the price of Berlin flights. He should make a to-do list. Of course there was the problem of the cash. That one would take some working on, but he was sure he would find a way.

Ned took out the red moneybox where he kept his personal stash. He hadn't looked at it for a few months. It still contained a vial of Testosterone Enanthate, a bottle of Nolvadex pills, some anti-bacterial swabs and a few syringes and needles of different sizes. He emptied its contents into a plastic bag, which he knotted at the top, left the house, and placed the bag in the same rubbish bin where he had dumped his hard drive last week.

Acknowledgements

Thank you to my agent, [illegible] and [illegible]; to [illegible] Murray; to Matt Angel, for [illegible] and [illegible] Parente, who each read drafts [illegible] suggestions; to Sharon [illegible] Katherine Angel [illegible]

Acknowledgements

Thank you to my agent, Lisa Baker, and my editor, Niamh Mulvey; to Mitzi Angel, Jon Day, Tom Marks and Daisy Parente, who each read drafts of this story and made helpful suggestions; to Sharona Selby, who copy-edited the text; and to Katherine Angel and Buddy.